D1180303

A Christmas Carol II

CONTAGION

CHARLES DICKENS AND BRUNO VINCENT

JOHN BLAKE

Published by John Blake Publishing Ltd,
3 Bramber Court, 2 Bramber Road,
London W14 9PB, England

www.johnblakepublishing.co.uk

www.facebook.com/Johnblakepub

twitter.com/johnblakepub

First edition 2011

ISBN: 978 1 84358 509 1

British Library Cataloguing-in-Publication Data:

A catalogue record for this book is available from the British Library.

Design by www.envydesign.co.uk

Printed and bound by CPI Group (UK) Ltd, Croydon, CR0 4YY

1 3 5 7 9 10 8 6 4 2

Papers used by John Blake Publishing are natural,
recyclable products made from wood grown in sustainable forests.
The manufacturing processes conform to the environmental
regulations of the country of origin.

AFFECTIONATELY INSCRIBED
TO THE HON. Miss DOLTON AND Mr. PEREPELKIN
OF WALTON-ON-THAMES, SURREY

God save us, every one . . .

VERSE I

Marley was still dead: to begin with. Of that, there cannot be the smallest morsel of doubt. He was quite as dead as a doornail. Deader, if that is possible, because having died he had gone so far as to appear to Ebenezer Scrooge as a ghost and there can surely be no better proof of death than that. If it is *not* possible, then the adage will have to do, and I will reiterate the simple fact that Marley was as dead as a doornail, and in his grave.

Marley had first died on Christmas Eve and then several years later reappeared on Christmas Eve, and as it was that very day today it can hardly be considered surprising that, when Scrooge sat by his fireside for his early evening rest, his thoughts happened upon that man, and on to the haunting for which he had so much reason to be thankful.

'I would be in my grave,' he thought, 'and unmissed. I would have no friends, least of all house guests (one of these, an American acquaintance, slumbered in the next room), and would not be sitting here in excited anticipation of Christmas Day, happiest of all feasts!' In a contented reverie, his ruminations roamed wider as he slipped towards a semi-sleeping state until they lay scattered all around him like a vapour. At last he fell into a sleep which lasted only a moment, for he came suddenly awake to a terrible groaning sound.

Such was Scrooge's acquaintance with indigestion that he was accustomed to being awoken by a fragment of his lunch or dinner getting into an argument with his insides, and between them making an uproarious tumult. He clutched his stomach, and saw that the fire had died to a pile of scarcely glowing embers.

'Good Lord,' he said regretfully, hearing a second deep rumbling. This was quickly followed by a sound like a heavy chair being dragged across the floor, and a most alarming sequence of squeaks and creaks. With his hands still to his side, Scrooge began to realize that he was in no physical discomfort, and that the noises were in fact coming from outside the room. A chilling supposition stole upon him. The noises grew still louder, and became an arrhythmic clumping as of someone dragging themselves up the stairs with a great exertion and clumsiness.

'I was in this very chair,' he whispered. 'And it was on this very night. Not another visitation!'

The noises stopped, as though whoever was there had reached the top of the stairs in a state of exhaustion, and paused to regain their strength. Unable to wait a moment longer to see what stood outside, with a great burst of energy Scrooge rushed to his door and pulled it open.

Before him stood a figure hard to make out in the candlelight. No ghost, but a thing of flesh and bone, its thin and frail shoulders were slumped, its features as grey as dust, and rags hung from its legs. At first he did not know it, and thought a near-dead destitute had clambered in through a window. He took a step forward to address it, but hesitated. There was something in its gait unearthly, and yet recognizable. Scrooge's first feeling of relief at not being once more confronted with Marley's ghost sharpened to a fresher fear. He saw the decayed features before him were indeed those of his former partner, yet they were altogether more (or rather, less) ghastly than before – the flesh ashy and desiccated, no recognition in its eye or semblance of awareness in its shambling movement. Not Marley's shade was this, but his decaying corpse. Scrooge knew this could be no ghostly warning, but only a more awful messenger from a dread and final place.

'No!' he cried, trembling. 'It cannot be! Jacob, my old friend, have I not heeded your warning? Have I not changed myself, and become everything you asked me to be?' He tumbled to his knees and looked up into the eyes of the dead man, but they showed no pity, nor any glint of human feeling.

'This is it, then,' Scrooge said, looking at the floor. 'My hour has come and they have sent you, most reproachful of spirits, to collect me. O wretched, worst and most abject of all deaths, how worthy I tried to make myself, and how your countenance tells me I have failed!' He threw himself to the floor and lay there trembling from head to foot in a transport of supernatural terror, waiting for the awful hand to take hold of him, and drag him away.

'Scrooge,' came a weary voice from behind him, 'look out.'

Ebenezer stared up in confusion and saw a spade swing above him and smash into the apparition's face. There was the wet gravelly crunch of bones, and Marley's whole head twisted round on its neck, the features flattened and distorted, and emitting a low, startled groan. Under the weight of the blow, the body swayed on the top step for a moment before crashing back down the length of the stairwell, bouncing in a most elastic and ridiculous manner, and coming to rest in a heap on the rug in the hallway, with one of its legs sticking over its shoulder. Next to Scrooge on the top step stood his American house guest and business acquaintance, Mr Dwight Tacker, spade in hand.

'How extraordinary,' said Scrooge quietly, dusting himself down and feeling as though he had rather made an exhibition of himself. 'You can see Marley, and touch him too?'

'Seems that way,' said the American, walking past him down the stairs to examine the body. He poked it with his boot and the head flopped from side to side.

'What was this spade doing hanging on the wall in my bedroom?'

Scrooge replied without taking his eyes off the (now indisputably corporeal) body of Marley. 'It was used to bury – well, to bury *him!*' he pointed downwards. 'When he was first buried. I hung it as

'HOW EXTRAORDINARY,' SAID SCROOGE,
FEELING AS THOUGH HE HAD RATHER MADE
AN EXHIBITION OF HIMSELF

an emblem of the burying of my former self, and a reminder not to return to my miserly ways.'

'Okay, I've got no idea what you're talking about,' said Tacker, yawning. 'You have any whisky? I could kind of do with a drink.'

'Yes,' said Scrooge. 'That's probably a good idea.'

The explanation of how an American gentleman came to be standing in Ebenezer Scrooge's house and in a position to rescue him from the grasp of a macabre apparition is best accomplished by a brief account of Ebenezer Scrooge himself, in the years which had passed since the events recorded in a former history.

Jacob Marley's first appearance in Scrooge's chambers – that is, after his death – had provoked in Scrooge a most remarkable change of character. Everyone who knew him (which was not, it must be admitted, a very great number) remarked upon it in the strongest terms, because he had turned, over the course of a single night, from a very bad man into a very good one.

Before that Christmas Eve, he had been a morose, avaricious, squeezing, grasping man with no notion of generosity to any fellow soul upon the earth. And now he was open, kind and well mannered, with never a thought for himself when he could be doing good to others. It was the utter completeness of this change that his acquaintances remarked in him, and their remarks were so frequent that in due course Mr Scrooge became quite a celebrity for his well-known patience and good humour. Indeed, his fame spread first through the local populace and then abroad to other cities, so that to be a 'scrooge' became a much-used phrase to denote any man unduly welcoming, trusting and generous. People who had never previously known of his existence would cross the road to meet him, or visit his office under the feeblest pretext, in order to shake the hand of this celebrity, known formerly to have been the most miserable man in existence.

One unexpected result of his new notoriety was that Mr Scrooge found his small firm busier, and more profitable than ever – adding to his great bonhomie – and in due course he was forced to expand both his workforce and the sphere of his trade. From a mere counting house, the firm of Scrooge and Marley bought out some other local concerns which by great prudence of management (and scrupulous fair-dealing) grew each in their own right, so that within a few years his portfolio showed him to be one of the most profitable businessmen in his part of the city.

As soon as he became known as a wealthy man, certain of his peers had attempted (through invitations to dine at their clubs, and the application of grouse, fine brandy and obsequious praise) to inveigle him into their rapacious schemes. Scrooge always declined politely and walked home reflecting on the sad knowledge that his former self would have fallen on these opportunities with a slavering hunger.

It was on his return from one such meeting that he noticed the appellation 'Marley' rather brought to mind the less pleasant epoch of the company when he had toiled under his former character. At this point the sign painter was called out, and asked to erase it, the firm afterwards trading simply under the name 'Scrooge & Co.'.

As his influence grew, it followed in due course that foreign interests prevailed upon Mr Scrooge to invest in them, and choosing to do so he found that these shores were no barrier to his success. It afforded him great pleasure to buy his first company on American soil, and to reflect that business under the name of Scrooge now stretched clean across one of the great oceans of the world.

In recent years, accepting that he was far from a young man and wanting to devote as much of his remaining energies to charitable works as he could, he had deputed most of his responsibilities to his trusted lieutenant Bob Cratchit. Under the auspices of this sound man the business's growth did not falter and soon the day came when the childless Scrooge finally had the honour and pleasure of accepting Mr Cratchit as a partner.

Thus, the sign painter was called out again, and invited to over-paint the name Marley (which despite his best offices had never been rendered truly invisible, but had remained in outline, much as his spectre had appeared in Scrooge's rooms) with the name Cratchit. The firm of Scrooge and Cratchit was formed.

Shortly after this Scrooge learned that his agent in New York was to visit London on business of his own, and at Christmas time too. On hearing this, Scrooge wrote back insisting that the man be his guest over the festive season, as it would be his great pleasure to play host and show him the finest English Christmas that was to be sought. *Thus* it was that the aforementioned Mr Dwight Tacker came to be in Scrooge's house (he is in Scrooge's kitchen as we rejoin him), pouring a tumblerful of whisky for himself and his host, and sniffing suspiciously at his own glass.

'This isn't bourbon?' he asked.

'I'm afraid not,' said Scrooge. 'Nor rye, I'm sorry to say – they are hard to come by in this country. The Scottish and Irish kinds are universally drunk. I did try to – *what* is *that*?'

Tacker was holding up a large rifle, pointing it at the ceiling and staring along the barrel. 'It's partly what I wanted to talk to you about while I'm in London, Scrooge,' he said. 'And I'm mighty glad I brought it, if we're to be attacked by the awakened dead. Here, have a try.'

He handed it over and Scrooge took it cautiously, his hands still shaking after his earlier scare. He rested it in his arms like a baby.

'Not like that,' said Tacker. 'Lift it to your shoulder.' Scrooge did so. 'That's right. Now, put your cheek to the barrel and look along it. See that picture over the fireplace?'

11

'That's my mother,' said Scrooge, his mouth squeezed against the gun's stock.

'Like her much?'

'Not particularly.'

'Okay, aim at that then. Now curl your finger around the trigger. Line up the sight – that's the little feller on the end of the barrel, see? Line that up with the tip of your mother's nose.'

'Got it.'

'Now *squeeze* the trigger gently. No sharp movements or you'll miss.'

Scrooge smiled at the role-play they were enacting and then jumped backwards in his seat as an enormous report filled the room, echoing deafeningly between its close walls. The picture burst from the wall, its empty frame fell to the floor and the rest of its contents showered over them in burnt fragments. Scrooge stood up, holding the gun and staring at it, speechless.

'Feels good, doesn't it?' asked Tacker, just as a high-pitched scream came from behind them. Both men turned to see a young man dressed in the solemn attire of a footman, white-faced and staring ahead of himself in shock.

'It's another one!' said Tacker. 'Scrooge – hand me the gun!'

'No! No!' screeched the man, waving his arms and shutting his eyes tight. 'Please! I'm not!'

'Don't worry, Tacker, this is my manservant, Damble.' Scrooge now turned to address his employee, and a minutely discernible change came over his countenance. His hands tightened around the rifle and an unwonted severity came into his tone. 'Damble, I was under the impression that part of your job was to answer the door.'

The man nodded without opening his eyes, still terrified out of his wits.

'Then explain to me if you will how the creature at the bottom of the stairs came to be standing outside my bedchamber with every intention of scaring me to death?'

'I'm sorry sir,' said Damble, taking deep breaths to steady himself. 'As you are accustomed to take rest at this hour I took the liberty of going to fetch ingredients for the Christmas breakfast.'

'Which is cook's job,' said Scrooge.

'Please sir, cook's ill. Her daughter sent message she is taken with the fever that's been all round the streets. I was planning to make the breakfast myself, sir, if it pleases you.'

At this explanation Scrooge's fierceness died like a snuffed flame, and the more accustomed look of gladness and understanding took its place. 'Of course, Damble, of course. It was very thoughtful of you to do so. Please excuse my harsh tone. Sheer bad luck this thing got into the house while you were out. Unfortunately it has left a hideous mess in the hall which my American guest Mr Tacker ('How d'ye do, son?' said that gentleman) kindly dealt with for me. Would you please drag it into the coal shed and we will deal with it more appropriately on Boxing Day. And when we've gone out you can clean up this room as well. I had an accident with the gun.'

'Of course, sir,' said Damble, gaining possession of himself with difficulty, and leaving the men alone.

Scrooge watched at the door as it closed. Tacker looked pleased. 'That's more like it, Scrooge. I took you for a pasty little English fag, but with a gun in your hands you act like a man.'

Scrooge leant the weapon carefully against the table. 'I've never spoken to him like that before,' he said. 'It is most unlike me. He is a nervous young man and deserves better treatment.'

Tacker wasn't listening, but gulping the last of his whisky and refilling his glass. Scrooge sat down and sipped his with perturbation. Holding his right hand out and regarding it, he saw it trembled still, but for a different reason than before. It was the tremor of excitement and power from the explosion of the gun which had galvanized his nerves. He had never felt anything like it.

'What was that thing, anyway?' asked Tacker.

'In a strictly literal sense, it was my former business partner, Marley. He used to live in this house before I did,' replied Scrooge. 'But no trace of that man remains in the thing we killed. Or re-killed. He died more than ten years ago.'

'Is that true?' asked Tacker idly, filling his glass once more. 'Well, he's not very good at being dead, if you ask me.'

'Well, that's an understatement,' said Scrooge. 'Perhaps it was some electric disturbance of the nervous system. Maybe his grave was struck by lightning. I hear the damp clay of London graveyards preserves corpses hardly decayed, even after a score of years. But this is no conversation for Christmas Eve. I fear any further attempt to rest before supper is now futile – let us dress instead, and I shall have Damble call us a cab.'

'Good. This killing has given me an appetite,' said Tacker, walking to the stairs and stepping over Marley's remains. Scrooge walked round them and stopped on the second step, looking down at the blasphemous, twisted thing. Its appearance ignited disgust and loathing, but for a brief moment that thrilling pulse he had felt at the exploding of the gun returned. Then he turned and ascended wearing an air of perplexity.

At length the men returned in evening wear to find the mess disposed of, and a cab waiting outside. Both mentioned their ravenous hunger, and as they climbed into the box Scrooge assured Tacker of the delicious repast that awaited them.

'One thing,' Scrooge said as the cab moved away into the fog. 'What did you mean by the word "fag"?'

'Let me explain,' said Tacker. 'Take your man Damble, for instance . . .'

VERSE II

Gibson's Chop House was a discreet establishment, tucked away from the bustling thoroughfare of the Strand down a side street otherwise bereft of interest or landmark, and due to the secrecy of its location and the excellence of its fare all the more cherished by its regular patrons. In the cold weather its glowing windows presented a very picture of cosy contentment and Scrooge knew the food more than bore out this impression, so it was with a delicious anticipation that he held open the door for his new friend, and barely a minute later they were sitting opposite each other at a small table in the window, each sipping a glass of Madeira.

'Mr Tacker, may I ask your first impressions of our country?' asked Scrooge complacently.

'Scrooge, I don't beat around the bush,' said Tacker.

Scrooge said that the attitude did him credit.

'I say what I think.'

Scrooge commented that this was no more than might be expected of him.

'I'm a straight shooter.'

Scrooge asserted that he would have expected nothing less.

'My first impressions of England? It's gloomy.'

'That's true,' said Scrooge.

'Cold as heck.'

'Hardly to be avoided at this season, I fear.'

'And you know what, the cliché is true after all. You guys really do have unbelievably bad teeth.'

Scrooge smiled acknowledgement, exposing his own mandibles, which resembled nothing more than a decayed and battered fence in a hurricane.

'But I'll say this for it,' Tacker said. 'There's no d——Yankees.'

Not for the first time since they had met, Tacker's choice of phrase caused Scrooge some severe awkwardness. With inward regret he recognized that he should act now to prevent further embarrassment.

'Mr Tacker,' he said discreetly, leaning over the table, 'You are a Southerner, I see. But I must protest. That is not a word we use, in England.'

Tacker was quite abashed. 'The "Y" word? I understand. It's dirty where I come from too.'

'No, "Yankees" is fine. But "d——". If the expression of extremes is needed (although in the main we avoid it), it's much better to say "dratted" or "blasted", in case you upset the sensibilities of the easily offended.'

'But I can say "a——hole", right?'

Looking around nervously, Scrooge considered how best to break it to the man. 'Again, it is a word with a much harsher connotation on this side of the Atlantic. I should definitely avoid it. Any curse, in fact. We simply do without them. Odd, I know, but it is the habit of the times.'

'So I can't call someone a "d——"?'

'I'm afraid not, unless his name is Richard.'

'And p—— is out?'

'Unless administered by a doctor with a needle.'

' "S——", "f——", "c——"?'

'Please, Mr Tacker, keep your voice down, I beg you,' whispered Scrooge desperately. 'Simply try to refrain from uttering oaths at all, as far as possible.'

'All right, Scrooge. As your guest, I will of course

do what you ask. But I warn you if I'm woken up by your business partner again I'm liable to let out a "m————" and there's nothing you or I can do about it.'

Scrooge shivered and looked over his shoulder to see if anyone was in earshot. To his exquisite agony, the maître d'hotel was perched at his elbow, awaiting their orders with an air of noble suffering. Unable to prevent a momentary look of horror crossing his face, Scrooge at once suppressed it, and let out a nervous laugh. 'Ah, my good man,' he simpered. 'May we perhaps hear the menu?'

The day's menu repeated much too fast for them to understand, the orders of food and wine made in a confusion of guesswork and apology, and the maître d' at last sidling away wearing a rigid mask of disdain, Tacker (untouched by the mildest scruple at his foregoing outburst) at once got down to business.

'Mr Scrooge,' he said charmingly, a world away from his previous unapologetic tone. 'We are here to discuss business. When I showed you that gun, earlier, you were quite unaccustomed to it.'

'I was,' conceded Scrooge.

'And that goes for all Englishmen outside of the army, I suspect?'

'And the gentry. To my certain knowledge.'

'Well now, I think that I've got an exciting proposition that might change all that.'

'I'm all ears,' said Scrooge.

In truth, however, he was only *partly* ears, his attention being at that moment arrested by a good deal of whispering at the next table, including several audible mentions of his name, culminating in a female voice repeatedly calling that name at an increasingly loud volume, followed by entirely unignorable imprecation, 'Coo-ee!'.

Tacker had already ceased his sales pitch when he noticed the women, and now his attention was on them he singularly failed to discern Scrooge's reticence to acknowledge the call.

'They know you, Scrooge? They're trying to catch your eye, I think.'

Scrooge turned round to see three women who, interpreting accidental eye contact as an invitation, at once invaded the gentlemen's table with their good wishes and loud voices, and pulled their chairs up to make it a jolly feast.

It was a recent and not (he might under duress concede) entirely welcome development in Scrooge's public life that on account of his considerable contribution to charitable institutions, he was frequently subjected to the familiar attentions of near-strangers. This group in particular confused him, as two of the ladies who made up the party (although his nature would not allow him to admit it) might have been considered by a weaker man than he to be rather irksome, and yet the third he found so pretty and such delightful company (which he would never have confessed under any circumstances whatever) that he could barely force himself to say a word in her company, on any subject.

The females Scrooge presently announced were a bouncy, rose-cheeked woman of fifty or so, a slim and delicately pretty girl of around nineteen, and a very old lady who was neither taller nor more animated than the average tree stump, and who sat in uncomprehending silence throughout. They were attended by an extremely fat and serenely smiling gentleman known to Scrooge only as a man of vast material wealth and remarkable poverty of wits, who smiled unceasingly in the warmest and happiest of ways, and had never been known to say anything of any interest to anyone at all. It was therefore a more than averagely bemused Scrooge who made the introductions.

'May I introduce three ladies of my acquaintance:

22

Mrs Emmeline Twosome, her niece Miss Felicity Twosome, their aunt, the dowager Lady Crimpton and Mr Peewit, a millionaire. Ladies and gentleman, a business acquaintance of mine from the United States, Mr Dwight Tacker.'

Tacker bowed minutely, but before he could speak a beaming Peewit leant forward with a rolling motion and breaking into a wider smile than usual asked if anybody else at the table owned a hot-air balloon, as they were so very *much* fun? No one could think of an answer to this, and as they shook their heads mutely, Felicity, who had been staring adoringly into Scrooge's eyes since the moment she had seen him, perceived her chance to divert his attention, by jumping into his lap.

'Oh, Mr S,' she said with a joy so intense as to make her quite solemn. 'We received the books you bought at our little school this week, and I distributed them amongst the little darlings and we taught them all sorts of geology and history and trigonometry, such as I never thought they would have a chance to learn – and they wouldn't, if it wasn't for you!' She concluded this exclamation by spreading a multitude of kisses all over Scrooge's face and head, so that he didn't know where to look or what to say.

'Felicity is a teacher at a local Poor School,' commented Emmeline, who had not stopped looking at Mr Tacker all this while, but had allowed her gaze to roam over the bulk of his physique and his face which (she might have inwardly observed) showed no more softness than one of the great Rocky Mountains. Her eyes grew wider with every instant and had taken on a worshipping aspect. For his part, Tacker's eyes had not left Felicity since she joined the table. Scrooge had distinctly heard him mutter, 'That's one fine piece of a— right there', and had shot him a warning look. Thereafter Tacker responded to Emmeline's enquiries in an absent way (only serving to sharpen her desire for his attention) while trying to communicate to Scrooge his feelings about Felicity with a sequence of facial spasms expressive of the furthest transports of ecstasy, and explicit hand gestures.

'You seem so rugged and untamed,' Emmeline murmured to him. 'I suppose you've killed many men?'

'Yes,' said that gentleman. 'And women too.'

'Oh, you *brute*,' she whispered. 'And I bet you didn't care one jot. I bet you didn't give them a second thought.' A convulsion most expressive of deep disgust, but whose true cause might have been any one of a handful of more approbatory emotions, shook its way up her body, reaching its climax in an involuntary shaking of her head, as though she was trying to scare away a bee.

All this while, Tacker was mugging most violently at Scrooge from behind Felicity's shoulder, his tongue stuck out and twisting round and round, with his fingers held up for his tongue to work between in imitation of some kind of act which left Scrooge mystified.

'How fascinating,' said Emmeline, still staring at him. 'Is that some kind of Red Indian incantation?'

'Not so much,' said Tacker.

'It really is the most *extraordinary* amount of fun, a hot air balloon,' observed Peewit, not in the least disturbed by the lack of attention, but still beaming from ear to ear.

Felicity was at this juncture attempting to force Scrooge to confess that he was truly the kindest man in Christendom, and chastising him as awfully naughty for refusing to do so. This strain of conversation involved a great deal of wriggling about on his lap, and succeeded as it was by another shower of kisses about his cheeks and lips, Scrooge remembered again the feeling of the gun's discharge earlier in the evening and felt a most uncomfortable sensation about his midriff. To distract himself from this he stared over Felicity's shoulder at Tacker. The American leered violently back at him and made a gesture with his hands where the thumb and forefinger of one hand formed a hoop, and the forefinger of the other poked repeatedly forward and back through it, like a magician tucking an imaginary handkerchief into his fist, ready to make it disappear.

Bewildered by the behaviour of Tacker and Felicity, Scrooge was about to rise and make enquiries with about the whereabouts of their food when the attention of all was distracted by a commotion at the door. The maître d' hotel was remonstrating with someone who was trying to get in, but who was clearly too inebriated to speak. His increasingly heated words (which had attracted the attention of the entire clientele) were failing to have any effect and he was attempting to push the stranger back onto the street with brute force, when the man leant forward, and rushing past him, ran towards Scrooge and Tacker's own table. Not only did he seemed quite out of his wits, but to have his eyes on Felicity and be making his way straight towards her. Before either Scrooge or his American friend could react any more than getting halfway out of their chairs, in anticipation of they knew not what, the outraged maitre d' caught up with the intruder and clasped him around the chest. To which the stranger responded, by biting him in the cheek.

Several diners who had been halfway to their feet in readiness to help, rushed forward in a general outcry. The maitre d' staggered back with a look of extreme shock, blood streaming over the hand he held to his face. Half a dozen men (Scrooge and Tacker among their number) fell upon the assailant and with one swift movement ejected him heavily into the street. They followed him out and stood around him with the intention of holding him down while one of their number ran to fetch a policeman. What immediately became clear, however, was perhaps even more disturbing than the attack itself. The attacker showed no penitence, or even understanding of what he had done, but flailed, roared and spat, snapping his teeth at any hand that approached him.

The six men stood back cautiously and watched as the violent drunkard rose and, with a further snarl in each of their directions, half ran and half stumbled down the street.

The men slowly returned to their tables,

27

disturbed and mystified. The waiter had been helped to the kitchen where another diner, happening to be a physician, tended his wound. Even Peewit's blithe happiness had been momentarily replaced by a gaping perplexity, although his asinine grin took only a few moments to make a recovery, and he took flight in his hot air balloon again.

'That was not something for you to see, my dear girl,' Scrooge said to Felicity, and placed his hand reassuringly on her arm. She kept her eyes to the table so as not to dignify the horror they had witnessed with a reaction, but a palpable quake shook her at his touch. Scrooge gazed at her for a second, thinking that she was indeed a very dear girl and feeling a protective pride at her decorum, when his thoughts and his eyes alike were distracted by the dish of curried kidneys which was set down in front of him. Remembering his hunger, and meeting the look of the maître d', which was now one of tortured sacrifice, Scrooge set about his meal.

The little restaurant quite outdid itself with the food, which entirely devoured the attentions of all present for much of the evening's duration. After paying their respects to their companions and finding a cab for the journey home, however, the two men both sat silently thinking of the attacks they had witnessed this evening.

There was a thought just out of reach that bothered Scrooge, something he had been ignoring in his characteristic desire always to see things in the best light. Was it that most of his workforce had reported themselves too ill for work the last few days? Scrooge had been indulgently amused by their attempts to gain a few extra days' holiday over Christmas, but now began to wonder if it might have been genuine after all. Was it that? No.

Was it that Scrooge's friends had almost without exception abandoned the capital this Christmas? Many of them men of finance, umbilically linked to the city, and distrustful of anything outside it. As though they all sensed something of which they were afraid to speak. And all the streets had been emptier this Christmas as though London itself receded from festive excitement out of fright at something unnamed. Was it that, then, that troubled him? No, still not that.

The carriage slowing to a halt in a narrow street, Scrooge's eye alighted on the faces of a small roadside gathering. Some uneasiness stirred in him, and he felt obscurely closer to his revelation. One of the group took a step forward, coming only a few feet from Scrooge's widow, while the others lingered back uncertainly. Something about this man made Scrooge uneasy, although he did not know what. There was an inanimate stiffness in his movement and a blankness about the eyes. For a second Scrooge thought he would appeal for some festive alms, but the expressionless man simply kept coming until he was at the window, and a superstitious dread rose in Scrooge.

'He's one of them!' shouted Scrooge, hammering at the roof of the cab to alert the driver. 'Drive on! Drive on!'

Whether the driver responded at once to Scrooge's encouragement, or the blockage in their path moved, the cab bucked forward with a sudden surge of speed, the man's face disappeared from sight, and they were carried home at great speed. Staring into that dead face Scrooge realised he had seen this look dozens of times in the last few days staring out at him from the street-side, and if it was as he had heard (and dismissed as nonsense) that a mysterious disease was making men violent, then perhaps it had reached epidemic proportions. Yet over a few minutes the swiftness of the cab's motion and its gentle rocking had the natural effect upon his nerves and soon he was asking Tacker's forgiveness for his outburst. Alighting soon thereafter at his door, sequestered in the quiet of a deserted yard, Scrooge sought to apologize to the driver as well, but found him distracted.

'It wasn't your shouting that made us bolt, sir,' said the man, speaking under his breath even though there was no one around to hear. 'We was attacked at the same time by a madman who bit Devlin (that's me orse's name, sir). Bit im! Look at his flank, sir!' Both men stared to where the flesh had been gouged by teeth, from which ran streaks of blood.

Scrooge wished the man a safe journey home and went to pay him double fare before thinking a moment, and then doubling it again. He waved him off and turned in with a grave presentiment. What Dwight Tacker must think of London now!

'They drink too much,' said Scrooge. 'That's the only way I can explain it. The police will have a busy night of it and we will have a wonderful Christmas Day tomorrow whilst a few ne'er-do-wells languish in gaol, the worse for wear. A good night's sleep will clear this all from our minds – it's not yet ten o'clock.'

Tacker made no remark until they were ascending the stairs.

'Scrooge, you want a gun?'

'Thank you, but no. I'm sure I would only set it off in the middle of the night and upset myself.'

'Suit yourself, Scrooge, but I'm sleeping with a revolver under my pillow and I won't take kindly if you get scared in the middle of the night and want to cuddle up. Good night.'

Watching Dwight Tacker go into his room and close his door before he could think of a dignified and dignifying response, Scrooge reflected that whatever the man wanted to say, he always chose the most provoking method of doing so, and also that sleeping with a gun under one's pillow sounded like a recipe for waking up with neckache. He locked his own door, and double-locked it (which was not his custom), and a few minutes later was in a deep and welcoming slumber.

VERSE III

When Scrooge was awoken some time later by a sequence of strange noises, the good humour for which he was famous deserted him entirely. He ran his hands over his stomach as before, but knew it wasn't that. There was a definite and repeated noise coming from downstairs.

He hesitated before unlocking (and double-unlocking) his door, but Scrooge was at the point in a man's life when weariness acts upon him so powerfully as to make peace and quiet more important than his immediate physical safety, and he had no hesitation in stepping onto the landing to find out what was going on. Doing so, he held the lamp above his head, and peered down the stairs.

It was a certain clattering and commotion which had first aroused him and had been followed by a thumping, dragging sound.

'Damble?' he asked into the darkness beyond the lamp's reach. There was a snap behind him of Tacker's door coming unlocked and that man shambled sleepily to his side. What was it, he asked? Scrooge did not know.

A low, regretful moan came from somewhere in the dark hallway, and the sound of someone shifting on the rug.

'It's Damble,' said Scrooge. 'He's drunk! I can't believe it.' Tacker disappeared for a second and came back with his rifle.

'Hold that up,' he said to Scrooge, nodding at the lamp. Scrooge did so. There was silence.

'Damble?' asked Scrooge again. 'Are you unwell? I don't mind if you are, only answer me.' ('I do mind, a great deal,' he muttered to Tacker over his shoulder. 'I've been very patient with that lad, and—' 'Shhh,' said Tacker.) Something shuffled to the bottom of the stairs and let out a light moan, and then began to climb them.

Scrooge's staircase was very wide and very deep, so wide you could have ridden a hearse down it sideways, should you have any particular reason for doing so. He had never had reason to regret the opulence of this feature before, but as that something started to climb towards them, they had no notion yet of what it was, and once more he quaked with fear.

'Damble!' shouted Scrooge. 'Show yourself!'

'Shut *up*!' whispered Tacker, raising his rifle and aiming it at the centre of the region of darkness.

By degrees it emerged. At first only a shadow, then a vague shape, then the shape of a man. Finally they were able to see its face, which was featureless, and covered with wispy hair. They froze in revulsion as the form lumbered up another step. Tacker's aim wandered away from it as he stared. It was climbing on all fours, yet seemed to have no eyes.

With a sense of disbelieving dread, Scrooge recognised the rotting clothes, and the mud-streaks upon them, and uttered, '*Marley!*'

'M————!' said the American.

Hearing its name (or the insult directed at it), the figure stood up and shook its head so it lolled back on its broken neck and its eyes and mouth were visible. It continued its mournful ascent with its face sideways, as though it recognized Scrooge's voice, and was following its ear.

'How do we stop it?' asked Scrooge.

'I don't know,' Tacker said, and fired a shot into Marley's chest.

'He's dead, what do you think that's going to do to him?' asked Scrooge.

Tacker fired another shot, splintering the corpse's shoulder, to no effect. It kept coming. He fired once more but the blind creature stumbled on a stair, and the shot went over its head.

Nearly upon them, Marley's corpse lurched forward with teeth bared. Struggling to reload in time, Tacker brought the gun back up just as the creature's mouth closed over the barrel, its teeth biting it with a click. Both men closed their eyes as he pulled the trigger. When they opened them again it was at their feet – finally, irrevocably dead. Tacker looked out into the darkness.

'Damble?' he called into it. 'You're f——— fired.'

They repaired to the kitchen to furnish themselves with a reviving tot of whisky and to decide what to do. Shooting the creature in the head did indeed seem to have killed it once and for all. Scrooge's solution seemed the most satisfactory: they would rebury it, and make sure it couldn't dig itself out again. Scrooge motioned, Tacker seconded, and there were no objections. Thus they found themselves, within half an hour, carrying Marley's corpse through the quiet lanes.

The fog was close and freezing, restricting their vision to no more than twenty paces, so that they expected at any second out of it would stumble another creature, or worse, an officer of the law who would no doubt be most eager to enquire after their purpose. The snow was thicker now too, rendering the streets silent except for their own dragging footsteps which made a shushing sound, adding furtiveness to their grisly enterprise. Added to this was the fact that the cadaver insisted on making small deposits of a black gooey substance about every ten steps so that any local man or (more likely) dog coming across their trail might be stimulated to follow it out of curiosity to discover the prize at its end. Thus they walked as fast as they could in apprehensive silence, looking around themselves at every moment, although they met no one and saw nothing out of the ordinary.

Shortly before they reached the church the mist lifted enough for them to see a short distance down the side streets they passed.

'You see them?' asked Tacker quietly.

'Yes,' whispered Scrooge. In every alleyway were to be seen little knots of people walking slowly,

37

occasionally bumping into each other. Sometimes it was one person on their own, wandering at a lugubrious shuffle. They posed no obvious threat, and made no sudden movement – in fact to look upon them and feel afraid seemed perfectly laughable. Even so, without saying another word to each other, the two men picked up their pace to a jog.

When they turned in by the gate to the churchyard they saw that the church was still lit. Resting Marley's remains on a sarcophagus for a moment so they could relieve their arms, Scrooge consulted his pocket watch and saw that it was still not yet twelve.

'They're open for midnight mass,' he whispered. 'Let's be as quiet as possible.'

They inched between the graves carrying their load which, in its advanced state of decay and after being swung about by their exertions, looked as though that at any instant it might detach itself from its limbs and slither into a dozen pieces.

'Careful, careful . . .' said Scrooge as they attempted to lever it over the statue of an angel. This figure was finely carved in the pose of a gracious abeyance towards the heavens, however, and despite their efforts its upward-pointing hand became wedged in a most inconvenient cleft in the corpse's lower body.

'Lift it up,' said Scrooge, holding the legs over his head.

'I *am* lifting it up, but it sags down in the middle, for C——'s sake,' replied Tacker with an exasperated whisper. The moment he said this, a look of devout humility passed over Tacker and he let go of the corpse to ask the Lord's forgiveness for taking His name in vain, as Marley's body slumped over the angel's hand, its crotch uppermost and the limbs dangling downwards.

'Dwight,' muttered Scrooge, 'I suspect the Lord will forgive you the more readily if we remove Marley from this blasphemous posture. We're going to the Christmas service in the morning, and you can ask for all the forgiveness you want then. Come on, the grave's not that far.'

Tacker silently acquiescing, the two men returned to their labours with the additional zeal of those with the end of an arduous task in sight. Within a minute or so Scrooge said, 'Here!' and squeezing with some awkwardness between two tall gravestones they stumbled upon the disturbed earth of an almost entirely bare grave, marked with a plain stone no taller than knee-high, which was engraved with the word MARLEY and otherwise quite unadorned.

'This is the grave you got for your friend and business partner?' asked Tacker.

'It was what he would have wanted,' said Scrooge, looking down with a dolorous shake of the head. 'Seriously. He was an utter skinflint.'

'Okay, let's get it over with, I want my bed. How are we to do this?'

Both men examined the earth and felt again the chilling awe they had both experienced when seeing Marley's animated body for the first time. The ground had been burrowed out from below and at the side of the hole, handfuls thrown to either side in thick clods. It must have taken an extraordinary industry and strength which, glancing as they both now did at the ragged figure they had laid on the grass, defied belief.

'What's that noise?' asked Tacker.

'The choir in the church, singing a hymn,' said Scrooge looking up at the windows, distracted. 'If we push him down the hole head first, that would seem the best answer. That will make it almost impossible for him to get out if he insists on coming back to life again, and we can pack these sods of earth on top of his feet. Do you agree?' Scrooge turned back round to Tacker for his approbation and realized what the squelching, rasping noise behind him had been.

'*That'll* make it pretty difficult for him to climb back out, don't you think?' said Tacker, holding out Marley's dismembered arms.

Scrooge wanted to feel horrified, but tiredness and pragmatism overcame the emotion. 'Pretty near impossible, I should hope,' he agreed. They crammed the arms (folded at the elbows) down the hole first, and shoved the exploded head of the corpse after it, levering downwards on the feet like they were the handle of a spade. When he was nearly in, they hammered on his soles with their fists, and then jumped and stamped on them in turns until they were a good two feet beneath the surface. Then they kicked lumps of displaced earth over the hole and packed them down. When all was flat again, Tacker spread a thin layer of snow over it so that it looked roughly as before.

'A perfectionist,' said Scrooge, amused. Both men got to their knees and wiped their hands with clumps of snow, to clean the deathly smell and splotches of dried fluid from them.

'You know what,' said Tacker, 'that noise doesn't sound like any kind of a Christmas hymn to me.'

Scrooge straightened and looked up at the stained-glass windows of the church again, listening. Now that he attended to it properly, he found the sound was low and droning, more like a long and dismal chant with no trace of melody. He glanced away from the windows to try to locate its direction.

'You're right,' he agreed, 'it sounds more like vespers . . .' He jumped slightly as he heard a twitching, snuffling sound from nearby, as of a small animal moving in the undergrowth. It came from the grave beyond Marley's, masked by a tall, highly decorated marble headstone. They peered around either side of it and saw nothing save an undisturbed layer of snow.

'What is it, a rat?'

'I don't care, Scrooge,' said Tacker. 'That ungodly music is getting louder.'

Scrooge leant closer to the ground. The little noise was coming from beneath his nose, but he could see no movement. Then there was a tiny tremor on the smooth white surface, as though a heavy object had fallen nearby. A pale trembling little thing poked through the surface.

It appeared at first like the nose of a frozen but persistent mole, but was then joined by another, and

another, until four identical points were sticking out
of the earth, and were joined by a thumb.

'Oh dear,' said Scrooge quietly.

'Why, what is it?' asked Tacker from behind him.

'Nothing, nothing,' Scrooge said airily. 'Let's
go h—'

The noise in the back-
ground became suddenly
louder, no longer appearing to
come from within the church,
but from all around them. Yet
this was not why Scrooge
stopped speaking. There was
now also something wriggling
in the snow, in the grave
adjacent to Marley's, just a few
feet away. It was an arm, pulling
away handfuls of snowy earth
to make room for the shoulder it was attached to.
Looking around for a direction to run, the men saw
shadowy movements everywhere they turned. They
jumped up onto a table tomb a few feet away, and
the elevation afforded them a fuller view of the
surrounding graves.

In one, a pair of hands had risen from the earth
and were placed palm-down on the snow as though

to haul the rest of their invisible body up by force. Turning to look for an escape in the opposite direction, Scrooge came face to face with a cadaver blackened by rot not six feet away, arching its back out of the ground from the waist up, its mouth open in a silent scream, whether from the effort to extricate itself, from some deeper spiritual agony or from simple decay of the jaw muscles, Scrooge did not seek to discover. In every corner, shapes were scrabbling up from below.

The graveyard was rising. In unison, they ran.

VERSE IV

The two men described very different shapes. One was an oversized American, who at first glance might be mistaken for a handsome marauding buffalo standing upright and confined within a dress shirt and evening jacket; the other a very old Englishman who was not altogether different in appearance from an ivory-handled walking stick. And yet by some obscure law of motion – perhaps owing to the precise equity of their terror – they both exited the graveyard at the same exact speed, and within a few moments found themselves resting against the gate outside taking deep breaths, and a few seconds afterwards proceeding at a not much reduced speed down the street outside.

Soon, slowing to a walk and gathering their wits about them once more, they began to breathe regularly, and to appreciate that had they passed anyone in the street in the last few minutes they might have appeared a little foolish. Each began to murmur mildly termed accusations at the other that he had been mistaken, and had caused them to take flight needlessly, and each inwardly quaked with a vivid horror at what they had seen.

'Perhaps we only imagined it,' said Scrooge, his countenance flushed and his mood (in spite of, or perhaps helped by, his recent shock) invigorated by the unaccustomed exercise.

'I dunno,' grumbled the American, who had developed a pronounced twitchiness, and seemed uninterested in conversation.

'After all, this is the season of fancy and magical things, and perhaps we are affected.' Tacker picked up his speed as they neared a public house named the Jolly Butchers, and noticed a group of people outside who appeared dull-witted with drink, and able to do no more than groan. He took Scrooge's arm and guided him down a side street.

'A time for spirits of every kind,' uttered Scrooge the philosopher. 'And if the working folk can't indulge on Christmas Eve then what is the purpose

46

of the verb, to indulge?' His bonhomie was improving with these thoughts, and was having a noticeably deleterious effect on Tacker's mood, to which Scrooge paid not the slightest attention. 'After all, can there be any greater restorative than to wake on Christmas morning, and be surrounded by your loved ones in fine fettle, and by the joy and love that Christmas brings, so warm and cosy that it could thaw the frostiest heart, and clear the sorest head,' he said chuckling, which irritated Tacker more than ever, 'and what's more, with a fine dinner to look forward to?'

At this point, with Mr Tacker's temper considerably excited, he placed one of his spade-sized hands on the top of the little old man's head, and, picking him up by it, spun him round so they were face to face. Scrooge seemed not at all perplexed by this but dangled there happily, taking this manoeuvre to be a friendly New World custom of which he had yet to have the acquaintance, and saw no reason to stop talking. After he had continued parlaying his generous platitudes for half a minute or so he noticed the deep glowering aspect of his companion and, his speech dwindling into silence, he hung there affecting a childlike interest in what Dwight Tacker might be about to say.

'Shut up,' said the American shortly.

Unable to move his head, Scrooge's eyes swivelled left and right as though to see to whom Tacker might be talking, as it was clear that he himself had stopped speaking a while ago. Then the American's face moved so close that Scrooge couldn't look at anything else.

'These people aren't going to wake up tomorrow morning,' said Tacker. 'Or ever again. There's something wrong with them – some sort of plague. Can't you see it? It's all around us.'

'Oh, Mr *Tacker*,' said Scrooge indulgently, letting out a light chuckle (which rather than shaking his head, shook his body), 'you're reading too much into things. Christmas Eve is a time for all sorts of strange goings-on, and of course there is *some* regrettable behaviour on the streets, it has always been the w—'

Without moving in any other way, Tacker twisted his hand so that Scrooge turned a right angle to the left.

'What's that then?' he asked, directly into Scrooge's right ear.

A dozen yards away, a figure lay supine in the alleyway, as dead and pathetic as the detritus of broken furniture and mouldering foodscraps that nearly hid it. Scrooge's heart swelled and broke: another pauper who his charity had failed to reach in time, and who had died, perhaps of starvation, so close to the feast of Chr—

Then he saw what it was Tacker meant him to see. Not the body but another figure, half-hidden within the shadows, who only became visible after a few seconds. It was another person, someone holding the dead body close to them, and clearly keening for their death, for they clutched the corpse close. It seemed almost like a passionate romantic embrace. But as his eyes became accustomed to the darkness and his ears to the quiet, Scrooge heard the ripe, slippery sound of mastication, and saw the mouth was attached fast to the body's neck. As his own features registered the horror of what he saw Tacker spun him back with a twist of the hand so they were face to face.

'Now you understand what's going on?' the American asked.

Scrooge struggled to swallow. 'Couldn't this be an awful individual case? An exception?' he asked. Tacker breathed hard through his nose, looked down and thought for a while. Scrooge dangled and watched him, and only after a minute or so asked quietly, 'Can I get down, please?'

The huge hand released him at once and he landed with a cushioned splat on the snowy ground. The devouring creature in the shadows looked up for an instant as Scrooge got to his feet before carrying on munching away at his meal.

'We've got to find somewhere to hide, and very quickly,' said Tacker. 'This disease has spread through the streets unchecked, perhaps for weeks, because it's so dreadful that no one wants to admit it exists. All the sensible people have fled the city. It's only your blockheaded love of festivity (here he paused to tap Scrooge roughly on the side of the head) that has prevented you from seeing it. They're not drunk people we're seeing out there, they're diseased.'

The tap on the side of his head, which on such a frail specimen as a man of Scrooge's age, might have produced a bruise the side of an egg, in fact served to knock some seriousness into the genial old Englishman and he stood (rocking slightly from the impact) and reflected for a moment before replying with perfect sobriety:

'We have come a long way from my home. But my office is near, and if what you say is true we must go there at once. Mr Cratchit may be at risk, and we should warn him.'

Without pausing, Scrooge set off at a brisk pace and Tacker followed, encouraged at the old man's change of spirit, and cast a last dubious glance behind him into the dark at the dribbling, snuffling creature by the roadside still intent on its prey.

They darted from street to street, hiding in alleyways and ducking between doorways, feeling foolish when they saw the occasional ordinary person passing along on their business, women carrying baskets or groups of men laughing and shouting, but moving ever faster as they set eyes on small clusters of slow-moving people who seemed to be suffering the effects of a deadening drug, and scarcely able to make any human movement at all. Each of them wondered whether the superstitions they were contemplating could be true, and felt as though they were foolish grown-ups playing a child's game of hide-and-seek in a most lamentable manner, until at last they turned a corner and saw the building emblazoned with the name Scrooge and Cratchit. They saw the bright lights shining through the windows, the sturdy door standing wide open and a fast-burning fire visible beyond, so that the entire street was permeated by a generally warm and welcoming air emanating from within.

Nipping across the street with glances left and right (the way appeared to be clear in each direction) the two travellers found themselves inside a capacious office equipped with modern and recently varnished desks, each appointed with a comfortable-looking leather chair far more expensive than that usually afforded to the ordinary clerk. The desks, too, were decorated with small tokens of personal identification, whether it was a curl of hair caught in an ivory clasp, a cameo portrait of a loved one propped up against the books, or a favoured pewter mug (one of them engraved, Mr Tacker noticed, with the legend 'Another day in paradise!!!'). Overall it presented a workplace with a singularly relaxed and familiar atmosphere, and sitting above all this on a raised plinth was visible the bald crown of the head clerk and partner, scribbling in his ledger with fastidious industry. This was Mr Cratchit.

Sad to tell, the change in fortunes which had overcome Ebenezer Scrooge's company in the years since he had first been haunted, and which had produced in him such a wonderful revolution in his character, had not worked upon Mr Cratchit in the same way. His family, which had been large to begin with, had increased so much in size that he could scarcely recollect how many there were, let alone remember all their names, with the result that love them as he undoubtedly did, he was as liable to garner a moment's rest in his own house (as he said twenty or thirty times a day, at the top of his voice) as he was to levitate from the floor and begin gibbering in tongues, with holy flames leaping from his nostrils.

That is to say, he was these days short of temper. Worry lines had sprung from either side of his eyes and mouth, spreading in furrowing deltas to the further regions of his face. He had developed a sarcastic look, and splotches of irritable red skin spread across his bald scalp as though angry devils roamed there, searching for the way in to the brain and thence to the mouth to find expression in one of Cratchit's intemperate outbursts.

'My dear Mr Cratchit!' said Mr Scrooge, 'it is late on Christmas Eve! You must abandon your work, and get home at once to your family!'

'Oh hello, Scrooge,' said Cratchit, without looking up. 'Happy Christmas to you.'

'Not at home, sir, in the bosom of your loving family? And less than two hours until the bell of Christmas?'

'No, not at home,' said Cratchit, quite unmoved, his forefinger tracing the figures down a column on his ledger, and his pen marking the total beneath a line at the bottom of the page. 'I am dreadfully tempted, of course, to escape home and be driven out of my mind by that pack of rabid animals. And yet for some reason I remain trapped here in perfect peace and seclusion, with this orderly workbook for company, and no respite to look forward to but my flask of brandy and some bread and jam by the fire at the end of the day. It is quite mysterious to me,' he said, leaning back in his chair and placing his arms behind his head with a sigh of deep relaxation, 'whether I shall ever escape this infernal prison.'

Scrooge laughed in the uneasy way that men have when they understand a joke has been made but are not quite sure what it is, and patted Mr Cratchit on the back. 'My dear fellow, you shouldn't take every-thing so seriously. Oh, but I forgot to ask after Tiny Tim. How is the poor lad?'

Cratchit's relaxed demeanour vanished, replaced by his customary look of antagonistic ill-humour, and he cast a long slow look at his partner, appraising him from shoes to crown, and took a deep breath as though girding himself for an oft-repeated and difficult speech.

'Mr Scrooge,' he said mildly, 'you know Tiny Tim?'

'I do, sir,' said Scrooge, beaming it might be said with pride.

'You know that he stood a full six feet four in his stockings, by his thirteenth birthday – that his name is now as sarcastic as that of Little John in the tale of Robin Hood?'

'I recall that to be true,' conceded Scrooge.

'And that he is almost as wide as he is tall, all of it muscle, and all of *that* owing to your repeated generosity in feeding him, and giving him money and gifts over the years?'

'It gives me no little pride to admit it,' offered the older man.

'You know that thanks to this he became arrogant and spoiled, that he has run up a whole host of fines, thanks to his efforts to help produce a new race of Cratchits with milkmaids, parlour girls and female servants across the length and breadth of London?'

'I have had cause to regret,' said Scrooge, scratching his nose, 'that he has this one flaw—'

'You know that he currently resides in the Fleet Prison, for non-payment of debts accrued in a variety of Cheapside gambling dens? And that, as he is still a minor, the debts are mine also? That he is a ruffian? A villain? A vile rogue of your creation?

A bane upon my very life? And that, may God forgive me, I truly believe the human race would have been the better had his life ebbed from him that Christmas Eve long ago, and left us the memory of a pure and beautiful spirit?'

Scrooge had now become positively uncomfortable, and his ever-present smile had become very wan, as his eyes travelled around the room and searched for a topic that might allow him to become his genial self again without provoking another angry tirade.

For his part, Cratchit was for the moment a spent force, and shrinking back from his upright rageful pose back into his usual hunched-over attitude, he regarded the old man's refusal to hear the truth about Tiny Tim with a weary defeatism, and knew this was a conversation they would have again, and then again, throughout the rest of their acquaintance. Looking away in disgust, he noticed for the first time that they had a guest, and became rather self-conscious about his recent words.

'Who's the ape?' he muttered to Scrooge.

The American looked round. 'Dwight Dugglehorn Tacker IV,' he said. 'Pleased to make your acquaintance.' With that he raised the rifle in his arms, aimed it at Mr Scrooge's head and said smartly, 'Now for the second time today, Ebenezer, I'm going to have to ask you to duck.'

Cratchit jumped, unable to fathom the American's behaviour, and spinning round saw with a most horrid and unaccustomed shock that a stranger was standing in between himself and Mr Scrooge. He must have wandered in through the door behind Cratchit, and what's more he was reaching out to Scrooge in a most awkward and unnatural posture, as though his back was broken, or he was miming the shape of a tree.

The energy of their recent adventures was still in Scrooge's veins so, although he was an old man, he leapt to the floor quite acrobatically. There suddenly followed a cracking sound that reverberated devastatingly loud through the room, seeming to Cratchit as though it was an outward expression of the shock the stranger's appearance had caused to him.

The strange man was thrown backwards almost to the door as the bullet hit him, but landed still on his feet. He said nothing, and did not even seem surprised, but — most remarkable to Cratchit — started walking forwards again towards Scrooge. Cratchit looked again upon his visitors as though to wonder whether any of them were real, and if this might all be a fearful dream in which nothing made sense, and the next person to appear would be his Uncle Peregrin, with his wooden eye and striped cockatoo. He sat down quickly and put his hand to his forehead as the American strode forward, threw a blanket over the bleeding but docile stranger, wrapped him up in it, kicked him out of the door and locked it afterwards.

Cratchit's breath began to return, and the lights to stop dancing and tingling at the top of his eyes while Mr Scrooge rose and dusted himself off, looking for all the world rather excited.

'Great! My delivery arrived ahead of me,' said Tacker, at once forgetting the stranger outside and examining a large wooden crate which had arrived several days ago and had been standing in the corner ever since, attracting mystified looks from the clerks (the few who Scrooge had not yet dismissed for their holidays early, and who would shortly excuse themselves). At once the American, with a good number of colloquial expressions the Englishman had not heard of (and a couple they pretended not to have), began levering the box open with a hammer fetched by Mr Scrooge.

Cratchit's attention was elsewhere. The man who had been shot by Tacker (and shot so casually) was now standing upright again in the courtyard, the blanket discarded. He wandered around in a figure-of-eight pattern before noticing the light from the window, and coming slowly towards it. There were so many fantastic circumstances about him that Cratchit hardly knew what to be most amazed or appalled by. He seemed to feel no pain from his wound, nor to feel the cold that leaked in through his torn shirt. Nor, after a first outpouring from the wound in his chest, did he seem to be bleeding: the liquid which had come out was already and congealed into the consistency of treacle.

'I cannot be awake,' whispered Cratchit to himself, 'because I believe this man is not alive.' The spectre approached the window and now stood in front of it, reaching out with his arms, but apparently lacking the wit to climb (which would have been well within his corporeal strength, had he been alive) onto the window ledge to break in. Instead his fingertips drummed ineffectually upon the pane, which dull repetitive sound had an uncomfortable effect on Cratchit's nerves. He heard the noise of rending wood and then the click and snap of machinery being assembled behind him, but no curiosity could persuade him to move his gaze from the creature on the other side of the glass.

'Dead,' he murmured, peering closer at the dull swivelling eyes, skewed mouth, and the expression of slack stupidity. 'You blunder through the world, feeling nothing but a distant sense of woe. Insensible . . . joyless . . . no more than a stupid beast, wasting away until you're no longer there. My God . . .' he whispered with awe. 'You're just like me!'

This spell of macabre fascination had brought his face as close to the glass as a child's to a specimen of poisonous snake at the zoo, revelling in the apparent danger and actual safety. Yet before he could bring himself out of the reverie, in its frustration the creature threw its arms forth again harder and smashed the window in, so that Cratchit had to leap backwards and turn away. As glass showered on his back, he saw both the other men standing facing him. Scrooge held a smart and shining brand-new rifle, levelled at shoulder height, while Tacker held forth a double-barrelled shotgun.

'What's this?' Cratchit was about to ask, but decided it was instead a matter of greater urgency to duck and retreat to one side, to watch.

'Now,' said Tacker patiently, as the creature finally gained the windowsill by a jumbling-up of its knees and elbows, 'remember what I said before. Stay still until you're happy with your aim, take a deep breath, hold it, and ... *squeeze* the trigger.'

Cratchit regarded this approach as an unwarrantedly cool one, seeing as the dead man, now that he had broken the glass and gained the windowsill, seemed rather to have come alive in his deadness, and to be intent on consummating his siege and storming the fortress, and was baring his teeth in a most unfriendly and atavistic manner. The only thing stopping him was a downward-pointing spike of broken glass on which he had stuck his head, and which for the moment kept him confusedly fixed to the spot.

Cratchit's gaze passed from him to the others and back again, until there was an explosion, and much smoke, and considerable pain to the ears, and an empty window. Scrooge and Tacker walked over and looked out, and made disappointed humming noises.

'Okay,' said the American. 'Were you aiming dead centre at his heart?'

'I was,' replied the kindly old man.

'Then your aim is up a bit and to the left. Possibly the impact of the shot is swaying you, and it's a matter of practice.'

The immediate panic seemed to be over, and in the hiatus Scrooge endeavoured to explain to his anxious partner about the creatures they had encountered in the streets. To Cratchit it all sounded rambling and confused and more than a little insane. The only thing he understood was that Marley had, somehow, apparently come back to life, a fact that he did not meet with the incredulity it deserved, but only provoked the glum remark:

'I suppose that means I'm not your partner any more?'

'Don't be silly, Bob. We buried him again.'

Cratchit nodded gloomily, as though this seemed hardly to settle the matter, with Marley having been buried at least twice before, although he perked up when Tacker added:

'And I pulled his arms off. Here . . .' The American explored deeper into the crate and began to lay complex pieces of machinery on the desk in front of the two men, who watched in fascination.

'Now, I know it's not usual to make a sales pitch late on Christmas Eve, but it would seem that this is a special case. We might have a chance to use them this very evening. Gun ownership in America is far higher than in this country, and I want to change that.'

Scrooge coughed discreetly to cover the bewildered silence that followed.

'Why?' asked Cratchit.

'The right to bear arms is enshrined in our constitution, and I'm saying maybe it ought to be in yours. If you had one, that is.'

'I don't dispute your need or desire to own guns and shoot them off until you're quite blue in the face and filled with as many holes as a colander,' said Cratchit. 'In fact, I think it's positively to be encouraged. But why bother us with it?'

'I see it this way. We gave ourselves the right to bear arms to protect ourselves from the British in the first place, after the War of Independence. And you're still surrounded by them all the time! So you need more!' He busied himself with getting more guns out of the crate, rather amused with his own facetious logic.

'So is what he's saying true? About the dead coming to life?' Cratchit asked Tacker in a whisper. 'I just always expect, at his age, you know, he might be starting to go . . .' Cratchit made a looping gesture with his finger around his earlobe but stopped when he noticed that Scrooge was frowning at him, and pretended to be tucking one of his few remaining curls back behind his ear.

''Fraid so,' said Tacker, clicking two large pieces of metal together, shouldering the resulting contraption and with his spare hand unlocking and raising a sash window. 'C—— knows what's going on, but there are men in the street who aren't alive, and aren't dead either. And they seem to be eating each other . . . *Look*,' he whispered, 'here's one now.'

The other two crammed around him at the window. Indeed, in the small yard to the back of the building stood another man. He had the superficial look of one stupefied through drink, but there was a stiffness in his gait that was more like a puppet's movement than a man's. Still the two Englishmen were uncertain.

'How do you know he's not sleepwalking?' asked Cratchit, fascinated.

'Partly because of the mud all over his clothes and hands, which shows he just crawled out of the earth,' said Tacker. 'And partly because of this.' With that, he let off a blast from the shotgun on his shoulder. Both of the Englishmen jumped and shouted aloud in fright, and when they returned to the window saw that the man outside had been picked up bodily by the blast, and wrapped around a railing at the rear of the courtyard, twenty feet away.

'Now that's your Tacker Ten-Bore, probably a stronger weapon than is needed in your market, and pretty loud to boot.'

'Loud, you say,' whispered Cratchit, who was still shaking from head to toe.

'Pardon?' shouted Scrooge, putting his hands to his ears and checking them for blood.

'However, for you Brits, I have *this*,' and he raised a lighter-looking firearm. 'I've done my research and shotguns in Britain are less accurate, heavier and average out at roughly triple the price of our Tacker Twelve-Bore, a gun which is hand-made with care yet as consistent and precise as though it was machine-tooled. They never stick, and have a repeat accuracy up in the eighty percentile, unlike your English guns, which average fifty, sixty per cent tops.'

After Scrooge retired to fetch himself a glass of brandy and water, and to have a little bit of a cry, Cratchit said, 'Let me have a go.'

'So, don't hold it too tight,' advised Tacker, 'and follow the sight there . . .'

The dead man had been slowly unfurling himself

from the iron railings and now raised himself to full height, obliging Mr Cratchit with his aim. As he took two slow steps forward Cratchit levelled the barrel at his chest and fired. It was with a sense of excited satisfaction the like of which he had never felt before that he saw the body lift up into the air again and thump against a far wall. Cratchit stood back, his eyes gleaming, rubbing his sore shoulder.

'You'll get used to the recoil,' said Tacker, 'but a not unmanageable weapon, do you agree?'

'Let me go again,' said Cratchit greedily, his hands stretching out for the gun. 'I want to pretend it's my wife.'

'Let Scrooge take a shot first . . .'

'No!' said Cratchit, grabbing the gun.

'Okay,' said Tacker patiently, and as he explained to Cratchit how to reload, a fortified Scrooge returned to their side.

'I think it's an admirable idea,' the older man muttered, just at the moment Cratchit pulled the trigger, so that his shot went high and wide. Scrooge reached out for the gun but Cratchit pulled it back.

'Not likely – you put me off. I get another go!' He reloaded with sweaty fingers from the bag of cartridges Tacker had placed on the windowsill and aimed again. Scrooge made every appearance of having no interest in Cratchit's target practice whatsoever, but glancing out of the corner of his eye, and noticing that he was ready and just about to shoot, Scrooge happened at that moment airily to enquire:

'What sort of order were you looking for?'

Cratchit looked to the American. 'Dwight,' Cratchit uttered, 'he's trying to distract me on purpose. Stop him doing it!'

Scrooge feigned innocence and, holding his hands up, walked away.

'Can you get on with it?' asked Tacker. 'The dead guy's nearly at the window. You can't miss him.'

A loud report filled the room quickly followed by Cratchit's shout. 'Yes! I got his arm off! Oh my G—, he's still coming. Scrooge, quickly.' He handed over the gun, nervously reloading. Scrooge raised the weapon and aimed carefully.

'Get him in the head,' said Cratchit.

'No, that's what stops them, and we need him for target practice,' said Tacker. 'Get him in the b—s.'

Scrooge fired and saw the creature's right leg splatter at the knee, making him fall sideways.

'Okay, near enough,' said the American. 'Now, this is a superior weapon, it's our top-of-the-line product. It's twelve bore again, only single barrel, but has a hollow stock which holds ten shells, and you reload by cranking the handle here.'

Scrooge began to load the weapon, while Cratchit walked away from the window with Tacker. 'How many units are you hoping to sell?'

'Well, I've got lots of other people I'm pitching to. I'll listen to any offers.'

'What's your unit cost? Now, we'd need a ten per cent discount on orders in three figures . . .?' The two of them moved away, Tacker answering the questions and Cratchit thinking, pausing and asking still further ones.

Meanwhile Scrooge was getting used to the 'pump-action' shotgun in his arms. He found that as he got quicker at shrugging the shotgun off his shoulders and reloading, he also became quicker at aiming and firing with satisfactory results, and found himself letting off three good hits every ten seconds. He was also discovering that, while the creature he was shooting seemed not to suffer the slightest pain from being shot, its body did come away in chunks, and while perfecting his aim he had carved such a huge hole in the middle of the chest and side that (with his right arm extended and his left blown off at the shoulder) he looked more like a walking question mark than a human shape.

And yet after each blow, a dull consciousness moved back into those eyes, and the creature began its attempt to get closer, even more sluggishly than before, as leaden as someone who has just slipped for the third time down an icy slope, and is trying to climb it again with less hope than ever. It swayed there, with no legs to walk with, but just Scrooge's countenance in its eyes, and it slavered, and waved its only arm, and beckoned towards him.

'Good Lord!' said Scrooge, seeing those eyes more closely than before, and crossing himself. 'It's our cab driver from earlier on. Whatever this ungodly infestation is, it doesn't just affect the dead. The living can be infected as well.'

He reloaded his shotgun thoughtfully, watching the dead body try to drag itself along the paving stones with its one hand. Reaching the shotgun out of the window and pointing it straight down, he fired into the back of the head which exploded like a dropped plant pot, scattering its brown decayed contents in every direction.

Scrooge continued to stare down at it for a moment and when he was finally satisfied he sniffed twice, made a quiet harrumph, pulled his head back in and began polishing the shotgun.

With their practice session concluded, the three

men convened around Scrooge's desk. There they sat sipping different drinks (Scrooge a cup of tea, Cratchit a tot of brandy and Tacker gulping from a large tumbler of whisky as though it was so much ginger ale). They discussed figures and margins costs and sales, wholesale and retail, shipping expenses and excise duty, as businessmen always must.

As had become his custom, Scrooge was at pains to make his guest feel welcome, by making him a sequence of cash offers so over-generous they were sure to put himself into bankruptcy. And as usual, Cratchit had to rephrase these offers rapidly, and repeatedly pull Scrooge aside for whispered conferences, where he explained the economics of the matter to him, over which the older man had once had such a limpet-like control and which now escaped him entirely. This was, these days, their way of doing business, and it made an amusing spectacle for Tacker who watched with an amiable smile, his mood further beguiled by nearly two-thirds of a bottle of whisky, a volume which he had consumed in only slightly more time than it took to pour.

A deal was struck, hands were shook, a further toast was drunk, and the three men sat back for a moment, and noticed the clock which showed little more than an hour to go before Christmas Day.

They had no carriage waiting, and still faced the problem of the man they had killed – or killed again, or the *corpse* they had killed – to consider.

Their eyes all moved from the clock to the window.

'Am I right in inferring,' asked Cratchit cautiously, in the clear hope that he was mistaken, 'that you think there might be more of these ... I don't know what to call it. A ghost? A creature?'

'Unless Scrooge and I were completely misled by all of our five senses,' said Tacker, 'I'm afraid so.'

Cratchit turned to his partner, who nodded in grave acknowledgement.

'How many?' he asked.

Scrooge and the American hesitated, each reluctant to deliver bad news. 'From what we could tell, and we did not wait to inspect too closely, they are abroad in all the streets about here. A host ... An unknowable number.'

At this, Cratchit stood up and sat down, ran his hands through his little remaining hair and glanced in all directions at once, betraying every sign of great distraction. Tacker cut short these anxious ruminations by saying shortly, 'There's something about *you*, Scrooge, that they like especially.' He had been making Mr Scrooge uncomfortable for some moments by fixing him with a concerted stare, and that man's consternation did not diminish as Tacker expanded upon his theory.

'When that dead guy came in here, Mr Cratchit's back was turned, his neck exposed. He was quite defenceless. And yet, Scrooge, he went for you. And think back to earlier, in our cab. It was to your window that they all crowded, not mine.'

Cratchit became sensible that a doubt had been lurking inside him all this while, on exactly the same theme. 'That's right,' he said. 'It was as though he recognized you, or smelt something upon you.'

'Do you wear a distinct cologne? Or a particularly noxious pomade?'

Both of the Englishmen stared at him with such gormless incomprehension that he abandoned the line of enquiry. 'What's different about you, then?'

'He's richer,' muttered Cratchit.

'Now, now, my dear fellow!' smiled Scrooge, placing a hand on his elbow. 'If that is true this moment, it won't be for long. I am an old man, you see – and you know you are my sole beneficiary and will be well provided for in the event of my death.'

'That's *it*!' cried Tacker, leaning forward and nearly knocking the whisky bottle from the table. He pointed at the two men, one then the other, and momentarily seemed overwhelmed by the admixture of the drink he had drunk and the idea he had thought, so that he was struck into silence. The other two looked at each other, quite blank.

'He's a *good* guy,' explained Tacker. The clock ticked twice in the intervening silence as he hoped for them to catch on, before realizing he needed to elaborate.

'As I've heard it, this is a city of extremes. Of extreme poverty and riches.'

The two Englishmen assented.

'And of great moral extremes too – where there is great charity and terrible depravity, happiness and wretchedness side by side. Now think back, Scrooge – was *every* grave in the cemetery disturbed when we were surprised by our visitors?'

'It was hard to tell,' conceded the old man. 'We were both in rather a panic. But on reflection I would say, no. Perhaps one in six graves was burst open, or fewer. Had every resident got up to meet us I doubt we would have affected our escape.'

'Exactly. Something has happened, some dreadful imbalance or curse on the city. Perhaps through some kind of a spiritual disturbance, or curious mineral composition of the soil, a great number of

73

tortured souls have retained some semblance of consciousness. Somehow in the deep and dark places, the mistreated and downtrodden, the crushed, the forgotten, have come back to a semblance of life, to take revenge on us. They are given animation by their hatred for happiness, and for the living – and they have somehow developed an ability to see it. They are drawn to it, like a light. As we've seen, once bitten, an ordinary person is infected by the same condition. They become mad and enraged, intent on devouring their fellow man.'

It was a gloomy speech in all, and was made all the gloomier because the untended fire was dwindling to dim embers as he spoke, and, several of the lamps also running low, shortly after he finished one of them went out with a gasping *phut!* that made the three men flinch as one. The room was now dark and the street outside, still illuminated by gas, showed a group of shapes crowding the entrance to the courtyard, where minutes before the way had been clear.

The implication of Tacker's speech was so mighty that it first struck Scrooge dumb, and then after a moment's wider reflection startled him back into speech.

'*Good* people, you say?' he said.

'It's only a theory, but I would say perhaps *happy* people is closer.'

'Why,' trembled Scrooge, 'then our companions at dinner must be the most endangered of the entire species! Remember how that ravenous monster in the restaurant went straight for Felicity, earlier this evening, before it bit the waiter? Poor girl, and her aunt and the old dowager too! And, of course, poor Mr Peewit is the happiest of creatures as well. He is sure to be a beacon to these benighted creatures ...'

'So there's some upside, at least,' said Cratchit.

'Mr Cratchit, what am I saying?' said Scrooge, taking his partner's hands in his. 'Your poor family, of course – we must hurry to them at once, and help protect them.'

Cratchit took on a thoughtful air as he considered the suggestion. For the first time that day, something approaching hopefulness into his eyes. He was, it cannot be doubted, a moral man, a stout citizen and loving father, and only someone who did not know him might have supposed (as he cocked his head on one side and raised a contemplative eyebrow) that he was considering the death of several, if not all, of his family, in its positive aspect. We, however, know better, and can only speculate that some other thought took full sovereignty of his mind for those many seconds, which must remain beyond our power to guess. Either way, at last his obscure mental perambulations seemed to come to a satisfactory conclusion, and he said quite calmly:

'If happiness is what throws mortals into danger, I should say that the Cratchits are *not* in the most immediate peril. Indeed, if most Friday nights are anything to go by, at this moment they are trying to murder each other with broomsticks and china vases, and generally acting like Blackbeard's crew on half-holiday. I should say that one should feel sorry instead for any dead folk who try to approach those dozen or so screaming savages.'

'You have a dozen children?' asked Tacker.

'Or thereabouts. Besides,' he continued, having another thought, 'the house in Hampstead is as sturdy as a fortress, and should keep those terrifying creatures out – or in, I should say – for a day or more, quite safely. So, if you're right, our first thought must be towards Felicity, Emmeline and Lady Crimpton.'

'It's settled then,' said Scrooge. An air of unwonted seriousness had come over him. Whereas he had seemed quite light-hearted at the prospect of personal danger to himself, the idea of something bad happening to so innocent creature as the young Felicity had clearly not occurred to him before now, and at this thought his eyes narrowed, and his expression became suddenly so mean and certain and pinched about the eyes that Cratchit thought he detected a hint of the old steeliness that had defined Scrooge's manner so many years before. Looking upon this transformation he felt a chill deeper than he had felt when confronted with the dead man, but one that passed momentarily, as fast as Scrooge overthrew this change of mood and assumed his usual breezy manner.

'We must go out, and find ourselves some transport. Which of us must risk going into the street to try to find a carriage is something we should toss coins for, perhaps, Mr T—'

Both men looked round at the echo of several rounds of gunfire, to find the door open and the American gentleman vanished. Several more shots were followed by the sound of hooves and wheels on the cobbles outside, and a shout. They ran to the door to see the American in the driving seat of a cart with a whip in his hand, the hole he had just carved through the crowd filling in rapidly behind him.

'Bring the crate, for G—'s sake!' he snapped at them. They complied as fast as they could, dragging it to the door, but needed Tacker to get down and help them lift it up onto the back of the vehicle. This was all accomplished in the flashing of two minutes or less, but still proved to be not a speedy enough exit. On turning the cart within the confines of the courtyard, in the gaslight diffused among sleepy fog that had sunk down from the rooftops, they saw in front of them a dense crowd, almost a throng, blocking the entrance, and moving quietly and slowly towards them.

'It's unearthly,' whispered Scrooge.

'Okay,' said Tacker from the driver's seat, swiftly loading his rifle, and then pouring a fresh supply of ammunition into a dent in the skirts of the cloak on his lap. 'This is our first big test. You might think you're scared, but you're not. Because we're stronger than them, aren't we?'

Scrooge placed a fully loaded revolver into each pocket of his greatcoat and held a shotgun up to take his aim. He and Cratchit exchanged a look over the barrels of their guns. Cratchit shrugged.

'Er . . . y-yes?' answered Scrooge.

Tacker looked round from his seat. 'I'm going to need a bit more support from you guys on the morale side of things,' he said. 'Just overcome your gentlemanly instincts, and blow their brains out. Okay?'

Cratchit saw that steeliness wink again in Scrooge's countenance and felt it reflected now in his own resolve. 'Yes!' he shouted in response, and heard Scrooge do the same.

'Okay then,' said the American grimly. 'On the count of three. One . . . Two . . .'

He reached the conclusion of his countdown, and struck the horse with the whip so fiercely it could hardly have helped but let out a high whinny and dash forward towards the line of corpses at a gallop. In a second they were among the throng, bodies bouncing off the side of the cart, all three guns exploding together, once and then again. Showers of blood, scattered flesh and nuggets of bone jumped up at them through the smoke. It was a passage of gruesome horror as though they were momentarily in the midst of some demonic battle, smoke enveloping them so they felt they would presently be delivered directly into the consuming flames, and know no more.

Yet in the next moment the fusillade was spent, the cloud of smoke slipped behind their shoulders and fell away, the wheels no longer bounced over hummocks of crushed bodies, and Tacker was steering them down an empty street at a fine lick.

Scrooge dabbed a foul-smelling viscous substance from his cheek with a handkerchief and collapsed onto the hay alongside Cratchit, both watching the crowd recede behind them with a weird numbness. The dead men and women bumped against each other and searched around stupid and half-blind, quite oblivious to their fallen comrades, into whose open mouths and exploded heads they carelessly trod.

'It's their *slowness* that horrifies me,' said Scrooge. 'The way they creep up on you, careless for their own safety. They just keep coming, no matter what.' And he shivered all over.

'Where to, old man?' asked the driver over his shoulder.

Scrooge climbed into the driver's seat alongside Mr Tacker, and Cratchit sat to empty his weapons of spent shells and fill them with new ones, as Scrooge gave quiet directions.

'I only hope we get there in time,' Scrooge said quietly, 'that none of our loved ones are hurt, and that they all live out the night. Are you *whistling*, sir?' He turned to look at Cratchit, who had unthinkingly taken up rather a merry tune. Finding

himself under the scrutiny of his elder, Cratchit stopped, and removing the cheerful expression from his face, replaced it with a more appropriate scowl, at the cost of some considerable effort.

VERSE V

The rooms of Miss Emmeline Twosome and her aunt, the dowager Lady Crimpton, were located in the corner apartment of a vast hotel, on the edge of a fashionable square as near to the geographical centre of London as anyone could care to be. It was quite evident to anyone who looked up from the street below that they were not only exclusive but expensive too, and without doubt most convenient to all parties who lived within, being within shouting distance of the shops of Oxford Street, should circumstances ever reduce such gentility into shouting for anything at all, which was surely impossible. The location of the rooms in such a charmed locality, however, as the fourth floor of an hotel, which delicacy prevents the author from identifying, presented the three gentlemen who sat out side in their stolen cart with rather a wearying challenge.

The streets they had traversed in their ten-minute journey were disturbingly calm. They saw individual stragglers swaying in the road and small groups either clustered beside public houses or bent over together in the street, as though a crowd had leapt forth all at once to assist a fallen stranger. There was no other traffic upon the road but snow, and fog, and occasional clouds of smoke that told of fires burning out of control not far away.

Each individual might be but a lonely drunkard; each group might be a gathering of the same, or sober and concerned citizens. It was confusing to try to tell, and difficult too, for Tacker's whip kept the horse from slowing enough for them to examine each situation closely. Therefore the streets around them, and by extension the whole city, felt like a trap, where, lacking evidence of certain danger, one might feel inclined to relax long enough to find oneself in absolute peril and therefore one was permanently on edge. So, quiet as the streets were, Tacker and Cratchit trained their loaded guns left and right on every flap of a newspaper sheet or a pigeon's wing that was borne on the cold breeze. As they maintained their nervous vigil, Scrooge knocked on the closed front door of the hotel, half expecting to arouse the interest of some undead creature within.

Instead he saw a head pop up from behind a counter inside, and pop back down again, and then a body scurry out beneath it and unlock the door. The face which peered out was a pale one, belonging to a boy of no more than fifteen.

'Are you help, sir?' he asked.

Scrooge considered the correct response, which was of course that he was neither the char, nor the brass-rubbings boy, and no gentleman had ever stood being referred to as 'help' without administration of a clip around the ear firm enough to remain long in the memory of he who had said it. But he also reflected that time was of the essence, and some matters of form might be dispensed with.

'I think so,' he said. 'The two Twosomes, and Lady Crimpton. They're still here?'

The boy shivered. 'It's only them left. Them and me. I can't make them understand the danger, and I daren't leave them unless they come to harm and I get blamed for it.'

'Don't worry about that now. You have somewhere to go?'

'Yes, sir. My mother's, across the river. I've heard this plague hasn't reached there yet. I think I can make it across Waterloo Bridge, or one of the others. You've seen these creatures, sir?'

Here was the first stranger he had spoken to about the problem, and despite all he had witnessed, it still felt in some way like giving in, to acknowledge out loud what was happening. Yet at this point, it would be pure madness to deny it.

'Yes,' he admitted.

'They're slow,' said the boy, 'and I'm quick. I think I can dart between them. If you are happy about getting the ladies to safety I'll try it, sir.' Scrooge nodded and as the boy realized his duties were no longer required, he saw a look of reprieve come into the boy's eyes, as though he had been granted a stay of execution. He slipped out of the door and ran away into the street. Scrooge watched his fleet darting form for only a few seconds before turning to the other men and gesturing them to follow. He did not want to imagine the boy's meagre chances of survival compared to their own even slimmer ones, and so concentration on the matter at hand was the only sensible option. Cratchit and Tacker joined him, bringing their weapons and his, and locking the door behind themselves they mounted the thickly carpeted stairs to the fourth floor, all three pointing their guns around each corner even though they met no sound but their own hushed footsteps.

When they found the room, Scrooge knocked lightly on the door, and found to his surprise that he was nervous in a way quite unconnected with the monsters who might be gathering outside at this very moment. He discovered that he was touching his hair in a distracted attempt to make it look more presentable, and noticing that Tacker regarded him with something approaching a smug grin he felt quite ridiculous, and wondered what he was doing. When the door was presently opened by the demure Miss Felicity, and he saw a look of surprised pleasure cross her face, Scrooge suffered a second mysterious attack of nerves, and became quite unable to speak.

'Mr Scrooge!' quoth Felicity, taking his hand in hers. 'You are here because of what has been happening in the streets, I take it? You have come here to warn us, or help to protect us, sir?'

Scrooge tried to nod and shake his head and utter something all at once, and succeeded only in rocking back and forth and making a kind of blubbering sound. The girl did not notice, and taking his inarticulate idiocy for chivalrous denial, launched forward and clasped her arms around his neck. This she followed by inviting the three men inside and they entered, casting investigatory glances along the corridor as they vacated it, to check they were not spotted.

Once inside, the men discovered that the speedy extraction of the ladies to safety was going to be neither as safe nor speedy as they had desired. The table was laid for tea, and the two old ladies were perched on the edge of adjacent sofas. They watched as the one, Miss Emmeline, nipped at the corner of a scone and the other, Lady Crimpton, took a doddery sip from her tea that took almost three minutes to execute.

'My ladies,' said Scrooge, bowing.

'Mr Scrooge! We have a visitor!' said Miss Emmeline, getting to her feet, giggling, running towards him, pecking him on the cheek, and then talking at the other men delightedly without hearing a word that they said, and generally acting like a hen in every respect except actually laying an egg, before returning to her seat and talking to Lady Crimpton very fast.

'My ladies,' began Scrooge again, with no softening of the gravity in his features, 'I fear that you are not safe here, and we must take you somewhere else.'

'Oh please, Mr Scrooge, do sit down and have a fancy. They are of my mother's recipe, you know, which she wrote these fifty years past – but nothing surpasses them!'

'Indeed,' said Scrooge, sitting and allowing himself to be handed a plate in order to engage her attention, before trying again. 'I am sorry to interrupt such a pleasant occasion with such grim tidings . . .'

'Mr Scrooge is a great PHILANTHROPIST!' Miss Emmeline bellowed to her aunt. 'He's a very KIND MAN!' The ancient gentlewoman slowly turned her head and regarded Scrooge with a look as dim as though through the wrong end of a pair of dusty binoculars, and made a nod so tiny that it might have been an involuntary tremble of her neck muscles.

'Miss Emmeline . . .' he began again, and stopped to accept a cup of tea. He tried to speak, but her bright eye was fixed upon him in a quite alarming manner, and he perceived he was to taste it, before he could distract her from the topic. He took a tentative sip and, catching sight of the disbelieving looks he was receiving from the two oil- and blood-covered men on the other side of the room, steeled himself to interrupt.

'Miss Emmeline,' he said once more, firmly, but with a patient smile.

'You haven't tried the cake,' said the lady.

'I must persuade you to come with us—'

'It was my mother's recipe. DO YOU REMEMBER MY MOTHER, DEAR AUNT?'

Scrooge spilled half his tea into his lap, which made an immediate impression on his temper. He was beginning to feel a long-forgotten impatience rising within him, which made him inclined to haul Emmeline and Lady Crimpton from the apartment by their throats, yet a single glance at Miss Felicity, her artless simplicity and exquisite prettiness, stayed his temper at once.

'Miss Emmeline,' he began again, with a firmer tone than before, and finding that he was starting to smile madly from the effort to appear calm.

'She was a great dancer,' said the tiny ancient woman on his left, pronouncing each word with brittle precision.

'What?' asked Scrooge.

'Yes!' chimed in Emmeline. 'How she danced. The last-but-one King George was quite entranced . . .'

'That is all very well,' interposed Scrooge, 'but I must insist that we retire.'

'No,' Emmeline pertly replied, spanking him on the wrist, '*I* must insist that *you* eat your cake and tell me what you think of the recipe!'

'Wonderful balls,' mused the old lady.

'*What?*' said Emmeline and Scrooge, together, quite shocked. The old lady turned her head slowly to witness their confusion.

'George III,' she said.

'I really *must* insist . . .' began Scrooge again.

'When bathing,' the dowager went on.

'How naughty you must think us,' said Emmeline, 'to be drinking tea so late!'

Across the room, Cratchit's violent trembling had returned so that the gun jiggling in his hand looked decidedly unsafe to be resting there. (Scrooge could just about hear Tacker muttering, 'J—— f—— C——, I don't know whose head to blow off, his or hers.')

'Aunty,' said Felicity, 'I think Mr Scrooge has something very important to tell us. You know the noises we heard in the street outside?'

'Oh, fiddlesticks, Mr Scrooge isn't here to bore us with the habits of costermongers, Felicity!'

'But I *am*, Emmeline . . .'

'Wonderful balls,' said the old lady.

'He'd much rather have a quiet cup of tea . . .'

'I'm afraid I must tell you that we are in danger.'

'But you haven't *touched* your cake!'

Scrooge saw Felicity looking sad at her failure to collect her aunt's attention, and then looking over her shoulders realised he was in the same room as two men about to turn utterly murderous. He tried again with determination.

'We MUST LEAVE!' he bellowed at the old lady.

'Not without finishing our tea?' she asked.

'Not without *finishing her tea*?' whispered Emmeline.

'Yes,' insisted Scrooge, showing as much physical exertion in forcing himself to say so as though he had just climbed a fifty foot wall. It might be said at this point that he wished he was not in this position. 'We MUST,' he said. 'At ONCE.'

'Not at this time of night?' asked the old lady.

'Not at this *time of night*, Mr Scrooge, surely?' muttered a scandalised Emmeline *sotto voce*. 'It is not done!'

'But we're going to die if we . . .' he said weakly, and knew that if he finished his sentence both women would pretend not to hear it, as within the polite lives they lived, it simply was not comprehensible to be killed. He felt defeated, and catching Felicity's eye, took a deep breath to try once more, when Tacker came to his aid.

The American came to stand in front of the ancient gentlewoman on her sofa, upon which she seemed to rise no higher than his knee. He bent himself slowly until his head was level with hers, and in his red-faced rage he looked as though he might accidentally snort her up one of his nostrils if he took a deep enough breath.

'LISTEN UP, RAISIN FACE!' he bellowed. 'We're all going to be CHEWED INTO MASH in about SEVEN SECONDS FLAT if you don't get your pea-sized a— out of here and into our wagon outside. I don't care for *MYSELF*,' he continued, yelling even louder so that the old lady's hair was ruffled by it, 'but FELICITY here is a FINE PIECE OF A— and I don't want THAT TO GO TO WASTE, YOU WEIRD LITTLE SHRIVELLED MONKEY'S BALLS★. Okay, so come on, let's go.'

Lady Crimpton allowed herself to be pulled upright and guided towards the door, muttering

---

★ Editor's note: it would seem this colloquial expression was so alien to the Victorian demotic that it escaped censure, or censorship. This edition retains the original text.

something about wonderful balls. She hadn't the vaguest idea what the man was talking about, but hadn't been spoken to in such a vigorous way by a handsome young man since before the passing of the Corn Laws, and at the recollection she brimmed with excitement. Miss Emmeline, for her part, was so confused by all this behaviour that she bowed her head and allowed Felicity to lead her by the hand. Bob Cratchit had been watching the whole scene pass off with an increasing exasperation and clutching his gun too tightly, for as he saw they had finally removed the ladies from their seats, he pressed even harder and loosed off a shot into the crystal chandelier above their heads.

As these rooms were populated by members of only the lower gentry, the chandelier was a modest affair consisting of two hundred and eighty pieces of cut glass and thirty-six candles, and which cost approximately the same amount of money that Bob Cratchit was likely to earn in his entire life. Despite, or perhaps because of this, it is not possible to express in words how profound was Cratchit's pleasure to see the thing explode.

'How exciting!' said the dowager, who had only seconds before moved from beneath where razor-sharp shards now fell in a murderous rain, slicing

into the furniture, and not the slightest bit moved by the exposure, as it belonged to the hotel. She tightened her grip on Tacker's hand.

'Wonderful balls,' she said absently.

'You can't even imagine,' he said. 'I'll show you later.'

VERSE VI

Within a few minutes they had escorted the ladies down the stairs. There was some initial trouble with the elderly dowager, who was so excited by the attentions of Dwight Tacker that she kept finding excuses to turn back so that he would shout at her, but once they discovered her ruse, she was given the sweaty hand of Mr Cratchit, and Tacker was sent to the front of the party to scout ahead for trouble.

They found none, every soul having abandoned the hotel for the streets, and some further destination. It afforded them no consolation whatever to be in the hallways of one of London's largest hotels on the eve of the biggest holiday of the year, and to be in darkness, faced with empty corridors extending in each direction, and they hurried until they were out of the lobby and onto the street.

'Now,' said Tacker, leaning down for Lady Crimpton, who presented so small a challenge to lift, she might have stepped onto his palm and been carried in his top pocket.

'No, no, no,' said Emmeline. 'Now I must protest. No one must lift Griselda but myself.'

'You?' asked Tacker. 'You couldn't lift a grapefruit. Come on, let me.'

'*NO!*' shrieked the gentlewoman, and raised her forefinger to admonish him on a number of points. 'We might be in an emergency, but the world is not entirely gone to pot . . .'

'Who the f——'s Griselda?' asked Cratchit.

'Don't you start swearing, Bob, you'll make her worse,' said Scrooge, handing Felicity up onto the cart.

'And what's more, this is not the appropriate vehicle for a lady to be seen in – or, or upon – under *any circumstances*. She should rather die.'

'Balls!' said Lady Crimpton, offering her hand up to Tacker, but Emmeline got in the way.

'Lady . . .' said Mr Tacker, who saw that they had gained the attention of some of the wandering creatures by the roadside, who were perhaps twenty feet away.

'No, it's not right,' said Emmeline.

'Shut up and hurry,' said Tacker, as he heard Cratchit and Scrooge loading their guns. More of the roving monsters were coming round the corner beyond. 'We've hardly got any time.'

'I'll lift her . . .' said Emmeline, bending to her elderly relative and placing her hands at the woman's sides. She made a lot of quick puffing sounds, as though she had taken a hot dish out of the oven with her bare hands and did not have a place to put it down (although she would have been thoroughly appalled by the analogy, as she had never been in the same room as an oven). By the time she gave up and the men realized she most definitely needed help, not ten feet behind her was tottering an enormous bearded man with a bald head, who might once have been a human cannonball in the circus, but was now an inhuman creature with his dead eyes upon her.

Scrooge fired, and a seam opened up from above the man's right eye and across the top of his head, so that a portion of his skull was either shaken loose or shattered within the skin, and the wound slumped open horribly, like a pie or pastry that had been roughly torn open.

The shock of the blast and this horrible sight did something unfortunate to Miss Emmeline's nerves. She turned away from the sight of Mr Scrooge firing the gun; she was confronted by the man's head falling apart; and she herself fell apart. She started a few words or sentences one after the other, and failed to make proper use of any of them, and while the men on the bed of the cart were still hesitating to come to her aid, another figure moved in on the little old lady to her side. It was a tubby little man, his arms reaching out, and he got to within a few feet of the dowager before Tacker deployed one rifled round through his left cheek, and then another through the centre of his nose, declaring, 'Hey, she's mine!'

At every second that followed the men wanted to jump off the back of the cart and gather the ladies up, but they had no sooner dealt with one encroaching figure when another appeared, and their activity was drawing attention from the surrounding streets.

'Come on!' shouted first Tacker and then Scrooge, holding out their hands to the ladies who were only just out of reach, before having to take to their rifles again. 'Grab our hands! Get on board!'

It was too late. There were too many of them for the men to help. One lady was too insensible from nerves to help herself, and the other was too insensible to anything to be of any assistance to herself or others. As the men realized this, Cratchit, holding the reins in his hands, decided that waiting any longer meant none of them would escape, as the creatures were getting uncomfortably close to the horses, and he whipped them to go.

'No!' cried Felicity as the cart lurched forward, and she saw the first monster bite down on her aunt's shoulder. The attack was swift and merciless, but mercifully swift. Emmeline registered no more horror at being bitten than she had in the preceding twenty minutes' horrors. The little old lady looked rapturously up at Tacker's receding form as the creatures set upon her. What followed was gruesome indeed.

The creatures were dead, yet they had strength, and they pulled the women apart like the carcases of cooked chickens after a Sunday lunch. Blood burst out of bitten-open veins and arteries, eyes were pulled out, loose things such as limbs torn away as more moving dead joined the throng, and

BLOOD BURST OUT OF BITTEN-OPEN VEINS
AND ARTERIES, EYES WERE PULLED OUT,
LOOSE THINGS SUCH AS LIMBS TORN AWAY

the voices of the women were very quickly lost as the cart dodged left and right through the crowd that had gathered, Scrooge and Tacker firing from each side to clear the way. Once they had broken free, both looked back to see only a feeding frenzy upon the road behind.

Quiet descended between them once more as the cart rattled away down a dingy side street, and holding Felicity to him, and absorbing the shaking of her sobs into his breast and the wetness of her tears into his silk neck-tie, despite the horror they had just endured, Scrooge found himself light-headed at his closeness to the young girl. Casting around for a cheerful distraction from their present plight, he settled on a topic that he thought would surely lighten the situation.

'Mr Cratchit,' he said. 'Tiny Tim. How *is* he, sir?'

Cratchit turned a grime-smeared face to his and

regarded the blithely smiling Scrooge for many long seconds, his head trembling under the agency of some scarcely controlled emotion. Then he spoke in a whisper.

'Twice in one day, would you? I've got a *gun*,' he said, holding it up barrel foremost, for Scrooge's inspection. 'It's loaded. So don't *ask me that*. Don't do it, Scrooge!' And he turned away the better to get a control of himself.

Quite at a loss to understand this outburst (his memory being not what it once had been), Scrooge also looked the other way, and was about to start whistling a merry tune of his own composition, which might have proved a fatal sally to Cratchit's exasperated patience, when the cart very suddenly checked itself, throwing all of its contents human and otherwise up into the air and rearranging them in an interesting new composition, back on its surface. Picking themselves up again, and checking their guns weren't about to go off, the human inhabitants stared out into the road ahead to see what had caused them to stop.

Tacker had the reins in one hand and with his other was aiming his revolver at a tall shadowy figure who stood in the middle of the road. No creature of the undead was this: he stood still, his eyes hidden beneath a dark wide-brimmed hat, his form concealed in long black cloak, and a large physician's bag stood on the road by his side. He had one hand raised with the clear intention of stopping the cart, and having succeeded in this application, he retained his pose, which made the horses snort and clatter restlessly.

'Pardon my French,' drawled Tacker, 'but who the f— are you?'

The hat's brim lifted slowly revealing a wiry, alert visage with two bright black eyes that shone with knowledge, and a small twisted mouth.

'I am one who can lead you to a safe place,' he said, his voice betraying an accent, as though he had been removed many years from the country of his birth, and also a pedagogic exactness of articulation, that suggested a gentleman of learning, or a madman, or both.

'I suggest that you let me aboard.'

Tacker was not impressed enough for his aim to deviate from the centre of the stranger's forehead. 'We have company enough, stranger. I've got a cart here that's good and full up. Suggest you get out of the way and let us proceed to Hampstead, and you carry on your way too.'

The man lowered his hand, but still looked at

Tacker and his gun. 'You will not make it that far north. There are far too many of them there. I have a place nearby. Drive me there, and you can all be safe until morning.'

Scrooge was deeply impressed that this man had survived alone on the street among the creatures – the only such survivor they had yet seen.

'How have you managed to stay alive?' enquired Scrooge.

'Don't listen to him, Scrooge, he's a creep,' muttered the American.

The man became impatient. 'I am a man of science. I have investigated every kind of apparition, ghoul and monster on the earth. It is my life's work. But these creatures – they are something new to me, and I have been out gathering specimens. Come, we are all fools to stand here like this!' He looked around irritably and hitched his bag up to his chest.

'Allow me to importune you for a lift and I shall explain. If the explanation does not satisfy, you may throw me off!'

'Mr Tacker, he speaks sense,' urged Scrooge. 'Let's make our minds up as we go. Get aboard, sir!'

Tacker lowered his gun slowly, allowed the man to climb up next to him and, in order to express his feelings about the arrangement, set the horses off as fast as they would go, throwing the stranger uncomfortably hard into the wooden seat before he had had a chance to set himself down.

When their guest had gained a little composure, he looked them all over quite coolly, and unconsciously placed his hand on his leather bag.

'Sir?' asked Scrooge.

'You have been fortunate to make it so far,' said the stranger, nodding several times to himself. 'Yes indeed.' ('A—hole,' muttered Tacker again, whipping the horses.)

As he looked them all over, the stranger's eyes fell on the open crate of firearms, whereupon he rose in his seat, leaned over and admired them closely, making clucking and cooing sounds and running his spindly fingers over the shiny and impressive-looking weaponry.

'Not so lucky!' he said. 'I take it back. You are well prepared.'

'That's my stuff,' said Tacker, 'but it's not for sale. Not to you.'

'Either way, American man, I need it not,' said the foreigner loftily. 'For I wield a cutlass!' Making a rather unnecessary show of his swordsmanship, he now drew the blade which had been hidden in a scabbard beneath his cloak and flourished it above Tacker's head, causing that man to duck and accidentally direct the horses hard into a side street. An inn was on that corner, and a heavy wooden sign, bearing the encouraging legend 'The Jolly Butchers' and depending from a strut beside the upper window, did the inhabitants of the cart great service in attaching itself to the raised sword as they passed beneath, plucking it out of the curious gentleman's hand and placing it out of harm's reach.

It took Dwight Tacker a few seconds' struggle to get control of the horses once again and when he had done so, with his spare hand he took the stranger by the scruff of the neck and deposited him into the cartbed behind with a violent flourish and a complete lack of ceremony or warning. The doctor's leather bag followed, hitting its owner in the chest and robbing him for a few moments of his breath.

'What do you keep in there, anyway?' asked Cratchit.

At this question the scientist recovered at once from his injuries and the loss of his precious cutlass, and unstrapping the top of the bag, foraged around inside, meanwhile delivering this explanation:

'Now, you see, to examine these creatures I needed *specimens*. I am nothing unless I have evidence to study, so when this outbreak began, at first I watched what was happening in the streets, and then when I saw it was some kind of illness, some, how you say, *contagion*, I knew I must study it. I was lucky. Nearby in the street I discovered a whole leg . . .'

Without giving them the slightest pause to take in this information he pulled out an adult's naked leg from inside the bag and dumped it on Cratchit's chest. One toe caught on the buckle as it came out so that as it landed the thing was wobbling as though alive.

'Turn right here, driver! We are not far!' called the scientist sternly, before returning to his captive audience. As his enthusiasm took hold and his speech quickened, his grasp of English loosened to an equal degree. 'And then I zought I must travel further and find better specimens, because perhups zees ees *not* an unfection of skin und muscle und bone, but might have origins in ze bladder, or ze colon; ze lungs, kidneys, or – most like of all – pancreas!'

As he announced each of these organs he produced them from jars within the bag and dropped them one by one into Cratchit's lap with a plop, giving him too little time to react after each delivery before making the next one, so that at the end of his speech the little man was furiously juggling wet sacs and bulges of red-raw flesh, in a desperate confusion of wanting to get them off him, but not feeling able to throw them away in case they really were important scientific specimens. Felicity, who had been startled from her grief into paying the doctor close attention, threw herself back onto Scrooge's chest with a further series of convulsions for which Scrooge could only be guiltily approving.

'And ZEN!' shouted the stranger, standing and raising his finger to the sky with disregard for low-hanging pub signs (and clutching his hat to his head with his other hand), 'I thought about their behaviour, and saw that zees was clearly a problem of ze BRAIN!'

With this triumphant conclusion, he upturned the bag and out of it bobbled the six or seven brains he had hacked free from the bodies of the no-longer-walking dead, depositing themselves with a sequence of splats upon the other bodily organs in Cratchit's lap.

Cratchit, trembling worse than ever and his face

and arms smeared all over with unnameable substances, fixed the scientist with an unblinking stare and began to load his revolver without looking at it. Felicity's bosom shook with sobs. The scientist laughed madly at his own breakthrough before checking himself and offering his hand to Scrooge while saying in a little voice, 'But I must introduce myself, my name is Dr Konstantin Zaltzwick.' He then looked up, bellowed, 'DRIVER! STOP HERE!' and as the cart bounced at full speed over an obstruction in the road, was thrown bodily off the back, landing in the road with a painful cry.

The cart clattered to a halt twenty yards on and the companions looked back at the cloak-covered figure sprawled on the stones with every sign of having broken his neck. But he got up, slowly and painfully, and as he straightened his back they heard him mutter as though it was a personal mantra, 'Hatstands, I love science. It's so ex*citing*!'

It was all too much for Scrooge, upon whom the excitements of the day had taken their toll. Cratchit scrambled to stuff the contents of his lap back into the jars in the physician's bag without damaging them, Felicity tried to recover herself by the application of a silk handkerchief to her eyes, and Tacker let off his gun into the sky several times in anger at not being allowed to shoot the insane scientist. At the same time Ebenezer Scrooge heard the bells of midnight being rung far away and slipped momentarily out of consciousness, and into a dream.

THE FIRST APPARITION

At first, everything seemed to him quite normal, and he was not afraid. He woke peacefully in his bed and saw the curtains at first dark, and then lit at the edges by a wholesome brightness. It made him sit up and draw them back without thinking before he fully recollected what happy memory the sight had stirred within him.

There in the middle of the room was a shining spirit, who he knew to address as the Ghost of Christmas Past. Scrooge's first thought was that he had taken his last breath, and that here was his spiritual guide for his passing to another place. Then he saw in that hovering sprite a look of urgency and sadness. Still his first idea did not leave him, that he was in the grip of his final judgement, and he saw that all his energies in the last few years had not proved strong enough to overthrow his former wickedness. A mortal chill spread through him, and he became fixed by an utter certain dread.

He rose slowly and offered his hand to the ghost.

'You know me,' said the ghost. 'We have travelled together before.'

'You are the Ghost of Christmas Past,' said Scrooge.

'I am that spirit. And you know I have no power but to show you what has already happened. Your tears are premature.'

Scrooge soberly dabbed the tears that had accumulated on his face with his nightshirt.

'Come,' said the gentle apparition, 'take my hand. I have something to show you.'

Scrooge trustingly took the Ghost's hand and coming to the window they rose up and flew out of it across the rooftops. Clouds enclosed them, and as they erupted from the other side Scrooge could see they were in a time many decades past. He looked down on a slum of the most appalling degradation. Hungry and parasitical characters lounged watchfully at each corner while pitiful families starved, and babies cried against their helpless mothers' shoulders. Scrooge saw street after street of these desolate faces, ignored by their neighbours who had barely enough to survive and nothing at all to spare, dying by degrees from starvation of body and spirit.

Scrooge saw the attenuated misery of these drawn-out deaths, whole families unsure whether their bedridden relatives were yet breathing, and themselves too weak to call for bodies to be removed when it was known beyond doubt that they were not.

Scrooge and the Ghost swooped into other streets and there they saw people who were so debased by hunger and desperation they were barely people any more, but were mere starving animals. Scrooge felt a tear land on his wrist from the Ghost's gentle cheek as they watched the miserable creatures turn, in their ignorance, to eating their dead kin. They did so tentatively and with revulsion at first, but base hunger quickly took charge of their appetites and dispensed with all human concerns.

They flew swiftly over rooftops, years vanishing in seconds, and alighted on a scene even more gruesome, that made Scrooge feel mired by the filth of a shambles even to have witnessed it: the habitual eating of corpses among the very poorest, the deathly visage and mindlessness that had developed among the living who so frequently devoured them, so that they seemed perfectly imbecilic and like animated corpses themselves. At last they landed beside the body of a man who had been dining for years on the flesh of his brothers, and witnessed the quiet moment of his demise. Thrown down on the floor in the tiny barren chamber and long forgotten in the dust was a worthless scrap of paper which Scrooge at once recognised – a promissory note bearing his very own signature, the kind that in the old days would be brought to him on a daily basis to try and raise an increase upon the original loan, and which he would take great pleasure in turning away with carefully chosen words of such sympathy and encouragement as often reduced supplicants to tears, so that they had to be led away. Here was one such man, who had appealed to Scrooge as perhaps the last person on earth who might have helped him, and, that hope destroyed, now the same (or rather, a very different) Scrooge looked down upon him in his final moments.

At the instant of death there was no light going

out in the eyes, merely a spreading rigidity which bespoke the final collapse of the internal processes, long after the brain had ceased to function.

Scrooge and the Ghost clutched hands tightly as they saw the lips quiver with a last breath, and then stay perfectly still. In his direst moment of speculation, Scrooge wondered whether here might be the first man (although aged perhaps only thirty he was quite old in appearance) who had eaten *no other flesh but that of humans* in his whole life. Scrooge and the Ghost clutched each other once again, as they saw that in death the spirit had fled, but the brain commanded the body still.

They watched as the body jerked itself upright and bared its teeth at a child who had run into the room, and reached out its arms. The dead body understood one thing – its own irrational hunger – and nothing else. At this, the invisible pair spirited themselves away as fast as they could from the sight that was about to unfold, and flew over rooftops once more until they were beside Scrooge's own window, and then at rest inside it.

'Spirit,' asked Scrooge tremblingly, 'what does this mean, what you have showed me?'

The Ghost shook his head, too sad to speak.

'You have done good to me in the past,' said the

old man. 'I changed my ways. I will do so again, if I can put this terrible sight to some good use.'

'I cannot tell you,' said the spirit. 'I can only show what I must show. You must make of it what you can. Before the night is out, you will have two more visitations.'

'Dear spirit, I thank you,' said Scrooge. 'I shall strive to be worthy of your attention, although this is all so wretched and confusing . . .' Even as he said it, he felt the room turning around him, as though he was falling inescapably into slumber. His head swooned, and he slept – which is to say, he woke.

VERSE VII

Scrooge awoke from the dreadful apparition to find himself on the bed of the cart as before, with the others fussing around him to remove the trunk of weapons and Zaltzwick's bag of specimens. In their busy-ness they appeared not to have noticed that he had been asleep, and choosing not to draw attention to it himself he clambered down after them. The road fore and aft was quiet and empty for the time being and, shaking the sleep from his old head, he looked up at the building in front of which they had came to rest. It was a tall and gaunt structure, something between a gothic church and a large public school but more forbidding than either. It stood in the corner of a

small square protected from the nearby thorough-
fares by rows of peaceful dwellings in whose
window not even a single candle showed.

'Come,' said Zaltzwick from the doorway, and
as he followed Scrooge looked up at a large stone
arch, decorated with gargoyles and indeterminate
statues, that might have formed the entrance to a
small cathedral.

Joining the party within, Scrooge saw they were
all in a narrow hallway much smaller than the size of
the building had suggested from outside. It was
decked with the jaded trinkets of nobility: dim
paintings, suits of rusting armour and cabinets
packed with grubby stuffed birds and chipped
ceramics, none of which matched each other, as
though they had all been bought on a single day's
rushed perusal of a cheap antiques market. As they
looked around, somewhat unimpressed (Zaltzwick's
eccentricity and nationality making Mr Scrooge
doubt whether a good cup of tea might be produced
as he dearly wished, and making Tacker worry that
there would be no whisky to hand), Zaltzwick
closed and locked the door behind them. He made
no move towards any of the doors that led from the
hallway on either side but instead put his key into a
hole in the far wall, between a mounted moose's

head and a fake mahogany grandfather clock, and twisting it stood back to let them watch.

It was a most impressive performance. Both halves of the back wall of the tiny hallway swung backwards to reveal a vast stone-paved chamber beyond. No dusty velvet-darkened sanctuary was this, but a huge vault of science, brightly lit, and filled with the most wondrous machinery any of them could have imagined, had they been granted the leisure to do so, for a hundred years or more.

'It was a property bought by my grandfather in the last century,' said Zaltzwick, suddenly shy at these strangers seeing his private lair, and quietly proud of it. 'The contraptions are of my own devising, the exhibits all from my own collection as well. The science of the strange and bizarre has been my church.'

He said no more but allowed them to look around and see for themselves what he had achieved, and how he had spent his life. Seeing the rapt wonder in their eyes, he felt suddenly moved to tears that, after pursuing these endeavours alone all these years, he might have had others alongside him all this time, who would have accepted him and would not after all have thought him a freak, as he had feared.

'THE SCIENCE OF THE STRANGE AND BIZARRE
HAS BEEN MY CHURCH'

'You are one f———-up son of a b——,' said Tacker. 'What the hell is *that*?'

'A baby troll,' said Zaltzwick fondly. 'I captured him in Trondheim. He fell for the old sheep-laced-with-laudanum trick.' The glass jar stood twenty-five feet tall, and in the vinegar the monster's skin had turned brown. It was not only Zaltzwick who saw a kind of defenceless innocence in that creature which could have crushed a house with its fist, and which now stood with its boulder-like face packed as close to the glass as a pickled herring, its eyes shut.

Across the walls of the laboratory were spread other examples of equal curiosity. Strange long metallic instruments that might have been used for catching lightning, or scraping samples from the roof of a cave; the top half of a huge-skulled dinosaur sporting giant, hooked sabre-teeth; limbs, eyes, brains and organs of every description in jars. Candles were on every surface and a flickering light on the walls; spilled chemicals and cracked glass on the floor, across which they could hear creatures scuttling that could be rats, and which on reflection they hoped really *were* rats and nothing more uncanny.

At last Scrooge looked up and saw a monstrous spectacle above him: what looked like a whole blue whale, hanging by enormous hooks and chains from the bell tower far above. From this carcase huge swathes of flesh had been carved, as though it was no more than a leg of ham hanging in a butcher's window. Then it was that Scrooge realized what the long-bladed implements leaning against the wall were for. The others followed his gaze until they were all staring upwards.

'What's it for?' asked Scrooge.

'Lunch,' said Zaltzwick.

'Lunch?' they all replied in unison. 'For whom?' Scrooge added.

'Henrietta,' said the doctor, pointing downwards. The group now noticed that they were all standing on a giant iron grate through which they could see into a pit far below. Perceiving this, they became very still with nerves, and all at once became aware that the vibrations beneath their feet, of which they had been scarcely sensible, were in fact the snores of a very large creature. The doctor looked at his pocket watch. 'She's asleep now, but I'll have to wake her up in a bit. It's nearly her lunchtime,' he added, tapping his watch.

'Wh-what is she?' asked Cratchit, walking backwards off the grate, taking great care to go as quietly as he could.

'Oh, nothing really, it's hard to explain. She was a present,' beamed the scientist, his attention already on other things as he spaced out the diseased human organs he had collected on a dissection table, putting them roughly where they would be if they were inside a complete human form.

They all watched as the doctor began to perform cursory examinations of the human organs one by one, coming at last to the brain, upon which he lavished his particular attention.

'Thees,' he said, holding it in his hand and bouncing it up and down, 'is the key to the mystery. Let me explain . . .'

'Wait a minute, wait a minute,' said Dwight Tacker. 'Who the h— are you, and how do you know that we'll be safer here than anywhere else?'

The doctor nodded twice as he inwardly translated the question into his native tongue, and then looked around the chamber as though seeing it for the first time. He looked up at the eleven-tonne chunk of desiccated whale blubber, and down at the grating through which droned the snores of an obscure monster. He nodded again, satisfied that in all fairness, for someone new to this place, one or two questions might demand to be answered.

It is unfortunate, perhaps, that his history as a

126

lecturer in the sciences (admixed with a native affection for his own voice) led him instinctively to deliver his answer as though addressing a crowd of adoring acolytes filled with wonder at his finest triumphs, rather than a group of blood-smeared adults who were tired, armed, and frightened for their lives.

'I am Dr Konstantin Zaltzwick. A doctor of science, yes,' he began, thumbing one of the buttons of his jacket and speaking at the top of his voice, which he directed slightly above their heads. 'And for many years I have explored the frightening and the unexplained. Across Europe and Africa, Russia, the Far East. I have seen men raised from the dead by shamans with nothing but bunches of burning herbs waved under the nose, I have commerced with ghosts and demons, tussled with ogres, played the battle of the wits with vampyres . . . I have visited and spoken with alien tribes of Antarctica and have been in many, many other strange places that you would not believe.'

Tacker, while he might have been enjoying the talk enormously, was making no sign of doing so, and was instead loading the repeat-action shotgun on his arm with a series of what might be termed deliberately and threateningly loud noises, while wearing an expression of grim determination. Zaltzwick took note, and sped up his exposition.

'*These* creatures I have read about, but never before encountered. Certain tribes on the Pacific islands and the West Indies have encountered similar things, or induced a similar state upon living beings, and there they call them "zombies". Meaning, those who are dead, but still living. But in those places they are stupid creatures, the servants of evil witch doctors. Existing in a trance, and doing as they are told. What is happening now here in London, is something else. More *human* in its inhumanity, or more animal. More – how do you have – more . . . *animated*.

'I have captured living specimens, and tested them. And here is your bad news: they are not men. They know nothing. They do not recognize their loved ones. They want no food that is not human flesh which might (in theory, if they were not dead) sustain them. They have no urge but to kill and eat. Or rather: to eat, with killing as a by-product of which they are quite unaware. Nothing else. They crave only to gorge on skin, chew muscle and sinew, to drink blood and bile and serum (which he pronounced sair-room), and every juicing that pours from the human body. *NERR-JERR!*' The doctor

128

suddenly screamed this inexplicable pair of syllables into a mouthpiece he had unloosed from a hook on the wall. 'I have guests! Bring refreshments to the laboratory at once!'

This instrument was a remarkable arrangement comprising a horn or funnel to catch noise and a rubber tube that transported it into the wall. The entire group assumed that it either made him able to speak to someone in a distant room, or meant they were confronted with a madman, who conversed through make-believe toys with imaginary servants.

'*Hatstands*,' said the doctor, replacing the mouthpiece.

'Pardon me, doctor, hatstands?' enquired Felicity.

'My dear lady?'

'You appeared to say "hatstands". Would you like me to fetch one, or . . . more than one?'

'I most certainly did not,' said the doctor, quite delighted at the idea that he would do such a thing. He gave Scrooge a smiling frown, as though to warn him to keep careful eye on his companion's flightiness. Before Scrooge could say anything in her defence, the scientist continued in his former strident tone.

'Since I first noticed the attacks on the streets,

scarcely a week ago, I have been able to discover very little about them. Except, that is, when they try to kill me, which is regrettably often (in fact, all the time) and then I discovered how it is to kill them most effectively.

'See here,' he drew back a curtain with a flourish, showing a long cage filled with the corpses of these creatures that had been shot until they were almost unrecognizable. Blood and detritus were spattered everywhere over the floor and walls, and it looked like nothing so much as a slaughterhouse. Once again Felicity (who had been rallying admirably) threw herself on Scrooge's shoulder. He was beginning to get used to the warm sensation this produced in all sorts of places in his body, and, realizing that he had been standing near her on the off-chance that this would happen, became confused at his own motives.

While Zaltzwick's various lectures (the latest being on how to kill these 'zombies' which they knew how to do already) went on, Scrooge was not listening, but making investigations of a scientific nature after his own fashion, within his mind. The apparition had shown him the evil that had begun this curse, and how in his former guise, he had had his own part in it. Now that it was set in motion and upon the streets like one of the plagues of Egypt, he knew there was nothing for them to do but escape. Yet there was more to it than that, and knowing that the apparitions had chosen him for a reason, and feeling a shudder of danger at what he might be required to do next, he momentarily experienced that cruel, certain coldness that had once been his permanent state: he felt strong and angry and pitiless, that joyous release of fury which would enable him to consign another to death without a thought. He had been used to looking back on this sensation with terror lest it return and yet now it did take hold of him it was warm and exciting, and strangely connected to his feelings for this innocent girl at his side. He had felt it earlier in the evening for a moment when they were upon the cart, and had seen by the fright in Cratchit's eyes that the former clerk had seen it too. And he could not deny he had relished that fear. These were exactly the qualities he had had to overthrow to make himself Good and Worthy.

He showed none of this on his face, but remained stock still, his pulse beating a little faster. He was his old self and his new self at once. Both men did battle within him, and he did not know which would win, nor which he wanted to. Returning to the conversation, he vaguely heard the doctor say that the animals could not be killed, and discovered he was staring into a cage at a grotesque display of blood and guts. The old Scrooge took over for the moment. He squeezed Felicity closer, careless of propriety, and felt her tighten her embrace too.

'Killing them is simple,' said Tacker. 'You just shoot them, like anyone else.'

'Not so,' said the doctor quietly, as he looked down at the decaying mess in front of him. He fell into a muse, and muttered under his breath for a few moments. 'Hatstands,' he said at last.

'What?' said Cratchit.

'What *what*?' said the doctor sharply. 'I did not speak. Here, you see, I shooted the man in the leg. He shows no pain, but continues towards me.' He pointed to one particular spot in the middle of the general mess, which was not particularly distinguishable from any other part, but clearly formed the remains of a certain subject. 'I shooted him in the gut, and then the heart. No difference.'

'That's right,' said Scrooge, 'just like that man in our courtyard, Bob. Shooting his legs off made it harder for him to come closer, but didn't stop him until—'

'Until you shot him *in the brain*,' said Konstantin

Zaltzwick. 'That is it. Even if you shoot out the neck, so much that you leave just a head on the floor, the head will still try to bite you. Although, thanks to the severed muscles of the neck and jaw, quite inefficacially – how do you have it . . .'

'Inefficaciously,' supplied Scrooge.

'Inefficously,' said the doctor.

'Ineffi*caci*ously. *Shou*sly, you see.'

'Yes, I thank you. Effi*caci*ously.'

'Well, yes, but you meant to say *in*effica—'

Scrooge's pronunciation lesson was cut off by a deafening blast from behind them, where Dwight Tacker had discharged his shotgun over his head, with the result that everyone in the room jumped, including the servant, a short curly-haired man with a placid demeanour and a very bulbous nose, who had appeared quietly beside Zaltzwick several minutes ago carrying a tray heavy with drinks, and since then had been awaiting a suitable pause to discharge his duties, with an increasingly shaky arm (and rattling tray). Now, through no fault of his own, the dozen or so bottles dispensed themselves across the floor with a most energetic explosion of glass and liquid. The scientist peered down at this inconvenient distraction for a moment, pointed at his servant and introduced him as 'Nodger' in a dim tone that suggested this destructive behaviour came as no sort of surprise to him.

'He is Welsh,' the scientist concluded, as though this explained everything, before turning his attention upwards to the underside of the whale into which a pound of lead shot had just been fired. 'Ach,' he muttered, 'zis will give Henrietta the indigestion.'

The others paid him no regard but looked instead at Mr Tacker, who having gained their attention was standing with his shotgun held above his head, and swathed all around in gun smoke, his imposing stance somewhat undermined on account of being showered with scalded lumps of whale fat.

'I don't know what that word means,' said Tacker.

'Inefficaciously,' muttered Cratchit from the side of his mouth, 'means it's not working.'

Plucking a marble-sized lump of sizzling blubber from his buttonhole (and momentarily tempted to see what it tasted like), Tacker said, 'This standing around talking is driving me insane. *You*, mad foreign scientist douchebag. You're saying we need to shoot them in the f——— brain, right? And don't give me some long answer because I swear I'll shoot you in the b——s if you do.'

The doctor nodded slowly, as though afraid any sharp movement might set off the American's gun. 'So long as the hypothalamus is significantly damaged or destroyed. That is the part of the brain in the very centre of the skull, and seems to be the centre of the disease – please don't shoot!'

'That's it?' said Tacker. 'Even we found out more than that! Did you know that they're attracted to *happy* people more than others?'

The doctor seemed a little put out that his expensive laboratory hadn't furnished results that impressed them more, and although he tried to appear aloof to this new piece of information, he could not. It intrigued him too much. 'How is this?' he asked. 'As though the flesh of happy person tastes nicer, is that right?'

'Exactly. We saw it ourselves.'

'Then they really are possessed, and this is not a neurological condition, or some outbreak of disease. You are quite sure you saw it?'

'Definitely,' said Scrooge.

'How fantastical. They don't just want to kill us, they *hate* us, and what we have. Somehow all that hate became conscious, and powerful, and built up until it was enough to propel these creatures up out of the ground, in an outpouring. And at Christmas, of course! When else are so many happy all at the same time? It is a curse, a plague upon us . . .'

These cheerful remarks were having no very positive effect on Bob Cratchit, who hovered at Tacker's elbow, looking as angry, twitchy and distracted as a man who was driven quite out of his wits with fright and shock, and who might explode into violence at the mildest provocation. He digested every last word with a sickly gulp, staring with wide eyes and hunched shoulders, before saying slowly, 'But we're not going back out into the street, are we?'

'I would advise against it,' said the doctor. 'Most strongly. Believe me, I do not want to die this evening. If we had the sole keys to Westminster Abbey we would be less safe than we are here. These walls are almost as thick, and we have but one entrance. And no windows.'

'So what's the purpose of scaring us s—less with this display?' asked Cratchit, almost beyond control, a great deal of spit precipitating down his chin, and taking less care of his aim than one holding a shotgun should (so that the rest of the group shuffled left and right with every twitch of his wrist). 'Why don't we just *stay here* and *rest* and *wait* for the night to pass?' Luckily Dr Zaltzwick's footman Mr Nodger chose that moment to reappear with another tray of drinks and, ready after last time, he bent double beneath Cratchit's wildly gesturing arm without spilling a drop, and straightened with a contortionist's grace to proffer a glass of port.

The change that this beverage made upon Cratchit was remarkable for its suddenness and its deeply mollifying aspect. The instant he laid eyes on the glass he was greatly impressed by notion of the effect it would have upon his shocked nerves and, putting down his gun and taking up the drink, he seemed at once very grateful and not angry at all, and possibly even a tad embarrassed. The rest of the group were more than a little relieved to see some calm return to Cratchit, and each individually made note to keep an eye on him in case this erratic behaviour took greater hold of him later on (as each was sure it must).

Cratchit's words also made the doctor check himself from further explication of his investigations into the 'zombie' creatures and instead draw the curtain across the cage, happily shutting the blood and gore from sight for the time being. He led the group to one corner of the chamber, where glass vials and retorts bubbled with curiously coloured liquids inside them, and where there were scattered copious sheets of paper with diagrams and notes scrawled upon them. These Zaltzwick swept to one side to make room for the party to place their drinks.

'You don't have a . . . a drawing room?' enquired Scrooge.

'I do not deem it necessary,' answered the man of science.

'Nor a parlour, or lounge of any kind?'

'You are the first visitors I have entertained these fifteen years. I sleep in the cot by the corner with my blanky, Nodger keeps rooms down below stairs where he keeps his feelthy habits to himself, and we haff a kitchen where he boils the food. That is all I need,' said Zaltzwick rather loftily.

'Well then,' said Scrooge, holding a chair for Felicity first, before sitting down himself and looking around somewhat doubtfully as one does when casting about with difficulty for something to compliment. 'Well,' he said again, and coughed into his hand, and repeated his examination of the chamber, somewhat at a loss. 'Good *acoustics*,' he said at last, and then started when someone in the shadows at the other end of the room seemed to make the exact same remark.

138

Tacker and Cratchit were ignoring Scrooge's attempt to make light conversation, and having unravelled a leather cloth, they set about cleaning and oiling their guns, the one eagerly attending to a lesson in the procedure from the other. Peace of a sort descended upon the gathering, insofar as peace may descend in such circumstances (that is to say, when one's life is in certain danger, and the skull of a *Triceratops* is staring down from the wall a few feet away). Zaltzwick passed the time making notes on more of the scattered pages of his research. Cratchit watched Tacker intensely, unconsciously replicating his every gesture, including when he picked his nose and placed the resulting gruel into his mouth. Scrooge and Felicity drank their refreshments and whispered heartening remarks to one another about their chances of survival, and each tried to genuinely believe what the other said, for the other's sake. Each time he spoke to the pretty girl now, Scrooge felt that hardening of spirit, that return to the wicked and unyielding determination of his former years – that is, he felt that way towards all other things that were not her, and anything that would hurt this innocent creature. Each time this devil, this former character of his, made another appearance in his heart, he inwardly protested a little less, for he was starting to believe that without this necessary evil, none of them would live out the night.

These were some of the reflections into which he was abstracted, once their conversation had ebbed, and the girl dozed on his arm. And by degrees, lulled by the wine and comforted by Felicity's proximity, he passed once more into a state of dreaming.

THE SECOND APPARITION

Scrooge came awake in his bed to the sound of the clock striking one, and finding himself alert and not wishing to be surprised by any apparition that might appear, but rather to take initiative and to surprise the Ghost itself, he threw off his bedclothes, pulled the bed curtains back, and found himself surprised nonetheless, to be but in his unadorned room of old, with no ghost or any other person in it.

For a few moments he stood unsure of himself, and by looking around, checking under the bed, and in his closet, and up the chimney, he eventually became aware of a light emanating from beneath the door in the next room.

'Of course!' he muttered to himself. 'I had forgotten he did not appear in this room. Still, he was a jolly enough fellow, and I shall make him welcome.' Had he been awake, this hopefulness may have had some degree of self-deception, considering the general circumstances in which Scrooge found himself, and indeed the contents of the foregoing vision, but hopefulness being ever an admirable quality that thrives in the heart of all true men, it was with stoutness of heart that Scrooge pushed open the door to reacquaint himself with this spiritual acquaintance of old.

Nor was he disappointed, because he found the room as he had upon that Christmas Eve many years before. It was festooned with greenery and hanging red berries so that it resembled an Arcadian bower, and upon the floor stuffed geese, and pigs, and turkeys and game birds of every type wrapped in rashers of bacon, all garlanded with coils of sausages. Upon a throne in their midst sat his former friend, dressed as before in a green cloak and a wreath upon his head: the Ghost of Christmas Present.

Scrooge rushed forward to take the man's hand, his progress impeded by the proliferation of good things over which he had to step, taking care not to trip. The jolly giant's face broadened in a happy smile, and his arms were thrown wide in welcome, and he opened his mouth to make a festive greeting. Scrooge persevered onwards although he had to wade towards his old acquaintance, so keen was he to thank him for his past services (and also, in part, hoping to be praised for how he had changed) it amounted almost to desperation. His progress was too slow, and he seemed not to be able to reach the Ghost, yet it didn't matter, because suddenly they were in the room no more, but in the street.

A chorus of carol singers gathered around a door, on a quiet city lane.

'Why it's my nephew's house!' said Scrooge. 'Such a fine lad. They are sure to be well rewarded here. Yet he doesn't open, and he must be in!' The hideous wailing let out by the small singers was not immediately distinguishable from the noise made by the average carolling group, and it was only as he passed them and saw over the top of the songsheets they held up, the horrible drawn faces and lidless eyes, that he understood the true reason why his nephew had not opened to them. And he passed inside with the Ghost's power, and saw his nephew and pregnant niece-in-law, both terrified out of their wits, crying and leaning against the door, begging for it to stop.

Before he could ask anything or beg advice as to what he could do to help his nephew, Scrooge was whisked away again to the front of a theatre, ushering its patrons into the night still aglow with the evening's entertainment, smiling, asking each other about what they had seen, and repeating their favourite lines, and looking for a cab to take them home in time for midnight mass. For a moment the panic caused by the previous vision abated and Scrooge found peace in this sight, but then he noticed a few people scattered about in the crowd, blundering slowly, with dead eyes and grey skin, and he had hardly time to draw breath to try to warn the crowd (who would not have been able to hear him anyway) before the screaming started. And once it had started, the stampede followed in what felt like a few seconds. As it descended the crowd parted and Scrooge caught a sudden glimpse which tore at his heart, of a woman who he hadn't seen in the flesh for as many decades: his former sweetheart, now grown to late middle-age, pearls about her neck and every sign of a happy and fruitful life that had been lived without him. Until, that is, he saw the dead body of a nurse bearing down upon her, and ripping into her throat with its teeth, and (lingering longer than should have been correct

144

according to Ghostly protocol) the violent spray of blood into the ghoul's eye as it tore into the artery, so that Scrooge had to look away.

When he opened his eyes he was back in the slums, where he had been with the first Ghost. He was inside one of the little rooms he had seen before, and now, on Christmas Day once again, he saw a whole family sitting down to its festive repast. Laid along their rough table was an elderly member of the family who the others had contrived to weigh down at the neck and waist with timbers, and into its midriff they were all tucking with mighty appetite, head-butting each other out of the way to gnaw at the ribs, sucking the fluid from a stretch of colonic tubing as though it was a sherbet sweet, and once they had got through to the bottom of the meal, chewing greedily on the marrow-rich chunks of vertebrae. Throughout, the head that belonged to the body snapped its jaws and groaned terribly, its eyes thrown open in an ecstasy of anger aimed at them not out of pain or outrage at its own bodily desecration, Scrooge now realized, but out of jealousy, for the taste of its own insides.

'Enough! Please!' begged Scrooge. 'Take me back!'

And to his surprise he found that the Ghost obliged him with his wish. He was back within the room, in front of the Ghost upon its throne of meat and pastries and sweetmeats, as jolly as ever. Except now he saw a hesitation come over its face. He had not yet uttered one word, and as he seemed about to speak the happy grin became fixed, and the generous expression of the eyes became strangely hollow, more like a careless rendering that fails to catch its true likeness than the things themselves. The happy rustling of leaves around him and gay flickering of candles hushed, and what it was in the room that had been so welcoming, became most uneasy.

Scrooge stopped, nearly falling over a brace of partridge covered in a snowfall of oranges. A painful groaning came from the Ghost, and his arms seemed outstretched now not to embrace, but out of pain. The Ghost began to shake, and became a pale green giant, and then a white one. A great wriggling motion at his feet, Scrooge saw, was not from the action of his toes but because some of the plucked fowls and other animals were moving, and their heads were bobbing up and down, as though they were suckling upon them.

Still Scrooge did not understand, and continued to watch even as he felt danger cloak itself about him. The Ghost shook slightly and his green mantle fell loose, disclosing that his chest was half eaten away from behind and with acute horror Scrooge saw the face of an animal behind the ribcage, its jaws guzzling away at the soft tissue of lung and heart. Now he saw a whole deer – or, being slaughtered and skinned, a whole carcass of venison – had reared up behind the Ghost, and with its blind eyes wide open, was chewing angrily at his neck with cracked teeth. Blood sprang up the Ghost's legs from which the skin and tendon were being torn, and it began to shake as a change came upon it. Its skin began to darken once more towards a deadly grey, and the expression darkened too, became bleak and haggard.

It was almost too late when Scrooge felt the dead creatures swarming about his feet. The animals were turning upon each other with their mouths, frantically biting and writhing, and where between them had formerly been dates and figs and mince pies, were now maggots and rats. It came as a horror of the kind no man should endure, to be suddenly engulfed and trapped by the animals he most fears, in the murderous throes of madness.

He stumbled and fell, and ran for the door kicking with his feet and shrieking every prayer and incantation that he knew, which came rushing out

HIS GREEN MANTLE FELL LOOSE, DISCLOSING
THAT HIS CHEST WAS HALF EATEN AWAY

in an incomprehensible jumble of words and syllables that could have moved no higher being to his aid, had there been one within praying distance of that dark place, for the time it would have taken to untangle the sense of the prayer.

With a last glance back he saw his friend the Ghost, who was without doubt now reduced to one of those dreaded creatures, marauding on hands and feet through the throng, clawing and gnashing at the dead creatures as they did so at him. Scrooge propelled himself through the door, and slamming it safely shut behind him, found himself in welcome darkness again, and, his consciousness throbbing from the effort and the shock, he swooned quite away.

VERSE VIII

Nor did waking provide much relief to the old man. His oldest colleague and friend was sitting nearby, it is true, and next to him was an American gentleman of great stature and strength and a most admirable directness of purpose. Beside those two men was a scientist whose life's work it had been to understand the kind of predicament they were in, and in whose admirably fortified house (which was but the kissing-cousin of a castle) gave them protection. Then there was the beautiful girl who rested on his arm, still quite asleep even though he had started awake with a shock, whose beauty was such that it bestowed grace upon any who looked at it, by the mere connection of sight.

'If we're gonna die tonight, Scrooge, you'd better tap that fine piece of a—,' said Tacker in the background, but Scrooge having no notion of what this sporting slang might mean, it made no dent upon his thoughts.

No, despite all these things, there was no respite from the sense of doom that lowered over Scrooge, and briefly encouraged his worse self to a new dominance which he weakly struggled to repel. The reason for this was the *groan*. Having come awake suddenly, he realized that the others had not noticed the sound coming from far away outside that penetrated even into this deep chamber. It was a distant chorus that produced a sudden chill in him no change of temperature could induce.

'Don't you hear it?' he asked. The other men looked up from their lessons – Tacker was now teaching Zaltzwick how to clean, oil and load a hefty-looking pistol while Cratchit tutted scornfully over the doctor's mistakes, which he himself had been making scarcely half an hour ago. All three looked at him with irritation for a moment, before understanding came into their eyes. Felicity had gently roused herself too, and all now found themselves looking to the fireplace, wherefrom the noise was issuing.

'How many of them can there be?' asked Cratchit.

'I thought only a few hundred at first,' said Zaltzwick with an air of resignation. 'That was a few days ago, when I noticed the outbreak before the authorities had become aware of it. *Hatstands*. This evening, I thought four or five thousand. But that sound . . .'

That sound was a low howling, like that of a high wind heard through a thick door. Quiet and innocuous at first, and unnoticed for many minutes, it had built around them as might the fumes from an unnoticed fire, until it was too threatening to be ignored.

'It sounds like a million people.' Felicity articulated what they were all thinking: that they had never heard from a 'zombie' any noise louder than a low groaning, and therefore that it could not be magnified into such a sound without a huge concentration of numbers.

They had hardly been here an hour or more, but it seemed as though in that time the walking dead had clogged the streets and that, quite possibly, a huge proportion of the remaining local population had failed to escape, and been infected. Whether either of these things were true, or some innocent trick of meteorology caused the howling wind, it chilled the blood of its listeners near enough to freezing to make them temporarily unable to move.

The men remained in their seats, wondering at the noise and its implications, while Felicity got smartly to her feet and approached the weapons laid out on the table. She had been dazed, and more or less passing in and out of a swoon since witnessing the destruction of her two relatives an hour earlier, but a few minutes' rest on Scrooge's arm had revived her spirits, and seemingly awoken her in another way, too. As she turned over a Colt revolver in her hands and stared down the barrel, Ebenezer thought he saw a new awareness of freedom in the young girl. After watching Tacker and Cratchit do the same, she sharply flipped open the barrel and began feeding bullets into it, a vivid look of what might even have been excitement in her eye. This sprightliness, and the determined set of her jawline, seemed to say: my old life might be dead, but it was scarcely alive anyway, and if a new one beckons, I shan't meet it by sitting around and waiting to be attacked.

She searched around her person and found that women's attire was not nearly so suited to carrying firearms as men's. The men, their pockets weighed down with guns, watched her with a new appreciation, which was not lessened when she discovered a final resting place for the pistol within the grip of her garter belt. She snapped the cold gun snugly to her skin without the smallest element of self-consciousness. She looked up to find the men all staring at her in a rather peculiar manner and, quite uninterested in what their reason for this might be, she demanded of them:

'Where are we going next?'

'Nowhere,' said Zaltzwick with finality. 'It is insane to leave. We are quite safe.'

Mr Tacker betrayed not for the first time some discomfort at this idea. 'Doctor, we are safe here until the morning. I agree. But you make it sound as if in the morning's sun these creatures will vanish like so much fine mist. I can't tell why you think this is so. Will we still be safe here in a week, or a year?'

Tacker and Felicity exchanged glances that supported their mutual restlessness.

Zaltzwick noticed and sighed, already aware he was going to lose his argument. 'If we can survive Nodger's cooking, we have a fortnight, perhaps.'

'What is there, a million people in this city?'

'Higher,' said Cratchit. 'More than two million, I think.'

'What might just be ten thousand of those things tonight could be twenty or fifty by tomorrow, and double that the day after. Then we really *are* stuck here, waiting for death to come.'

These were calculations it had never occurred to Scrooge to make himself, and he felt a sharp constriction of his chest, as though a band had been stretched around it and was being wound viciously tight. His reaction was not that of a helpless old man, however. He felt that cold determination stealing over him again. 'Where shall we go?' he demanded.

'This is what I've been waiting to tell you. Scrooge and Cratchit is not the only European firm I was due to visit. Later I was due in Belgium, then afterwards Holland and a few other countries where we had already received orders for armaments. These supplies are on my boat, a freight ship of good size, and it's moored in the Thames as we speak. There are many tonnes of weapons, ammunition and explosives on board. If we can get there we can defend ourselves for as long as we like, and escape.'

Zaltzwick watched the growing eagerness of the group with sorrow. 'I have observed these creatures this last week while you were eating dinner, and having business meetings, and paying not the slightest attention. Although they don't die easily or quickly, they crave flesh *very much*, and move on to find new victims fast. The streets around the centre of the city are already overrun, the population has either escaped or is infected. Within a day or more, these animals will spread out into the suburbs. I am convinced of it. Some will remain, but most will flee, then it will be safe to make our escape.'

It is sadly a remarkable feature of groups under great duress that they listen to the opinion that closest fits their own preconception, rather than making themselves open to persuasion from one who sees a more uncomfortable but more rational truth. Whether this was the case with the party of fugitives within the great vaulted laboratory that night, is hard to say, but it seemed this way to Dr Zaltzwick as he watched his words fail to impress those around him. Some lingering shred of guilt or awareness that he spoke good sense made them avoid his eye, and quite rudely refuse him a response, as they set about arming themselves to full capacity.

Cratchit seemed especially voracious when it came to placing guns about his person. In this crisis his habitually nervous and irritable disposition had achieved a kind of apotheosis of its crazed condition: now, at last, what he had always thought to be true, irrevocably was: the world *was* out to get him, and he was most certainly not going to miss his opportunity to give the world back some of what it deserved. Which is to say, he had gone off his head, and was determined to die, and die fighting, and therefore when he stood he rocked unsteadily from side to side and his clothes clanked as though they were a lumpy suit of armour, cleverly disguised as cheap cloth.

The group made their way towards the door through which they had come, making as they strode away from him, Zaltzwick thought, a rather fearsome spectacle with guns over shoulders or swinging from their hands, and all walking with a stone-cold deadly purpose; four horsemen without their steeds, venturing into the Apocalypse; a vengeful posse. He started out of these ruminations as he saw them pass through the door into the chamber beyond.

'Please,' said Zaltzwick, catching up with them, 'this is not fair. You are risking my life, as well as your own. Come first up to the tower and look! We can see how crowded the streets are and decide together.'

'He's stalling,' said Cratchit, looking perfectly crazed in the shadow of the antechamber. Tacker looked indecisive for the first time. It did after all seem a fair request but his urge to action gave him pause long enough for Cratchit to state his argument even more emphatically.

'There's no point!' he said in the manner of a child dissatisfied at its own birthday party.

Zaltzwick looked to Scrooge and the girl for support and, noticing that for the moment they were both staring at Cratchit, he reached desperately for Scrooge's gun. The old man could not help but instinctively yank it back to regain control and with his hand still around the trigger, it went off. The shot passed closely between Felicity and Tacker, ruffling the latter's coat pocket, and as the shock and flash of the blast resounded in all their ears and exposed to them the danger of their own lunacy, in one moment they became united as a group once more. Two of them had just escaped being murdered and two of them had escaped becoming murderers. It was suddenly clear to them all that they must retreat into the hall, go up the stairs and briefly survey the streets, rather than stride out recklessly and at once.

They had scarcely a minute to contemplate this new enterprise, and to set out with great unity of purpose towards the stairwell on the far side of the laboratory, when this measure was rendered unnecessary.

There came first a minute and high-pitched squeaking, that might have been a mouse in extreme distress. They faltered; they stopped and looked at each other; they hunted for its source, above them and on every side.

The sound then graduated to a wooden creaking, a long ascending note laden with impersonal menace. They turned round as slowly as they dared and saw what in their haste they had not at first perceived: where the shot had gone. Fired at such proximity to the door, it had passed wholly into the beam across its centre, and the wooden structure (thick and ancient and made of dry strong oak) seemed to be taking a subtle change in shape. They remained silent, and watched. Cratchit raised his gun.

'For G—'s sake, not again, Bob!' whispered Scrooge, gently pressing the barrel towards the floor. They all crept closer in curiosity, and made out what now appeared to be a bulge in the middle of the door. The creaking grew into a splintering, and at last matured into a snap signalling some fissure in the vast oak frame, which now allowed another noise through. It was the Groaning. Another creaking splintering noise broke out, as another of the door's timbers protested under the stress.

They all looked to Zaltzwick, and in their eyes was apology, and sorrow, and the expectation of furious despair from that man. But he said quietly, 'It would appear I was right. And the gunshot has attracted them too. It is too late now to escape this way. Let us fasten the inward door, and make as good a defence as we can. I am still hopeful they will go away when they find they cannot penetrate this house.'

No voice demurred. They all retreated.

Tacker and the doctor at once moved to close the inner door, and find furniture and props to keep it that way for as long as possible. Cratchit and Scrooge's eyes met and the old man felt suddenly the same way his partner did: that this giant draughty vault, as large as a cathedral, was no more comforting than an airless prison cell. It felt like a tomb, now that they were trapped inside, and the stone walls, almost invisibly distant as they were, pressed against him as though they formed a coffin moulded to his form. He tried and found himself unable to take a deep breath. Once more the old Scrooge, the mean and grasping man, rose within him and this time the new, kindly, generous Scrooge, the Good Fellow who wished nothing but happiness to all his fellow men, welcomed him, and retiring, allowed the scoundrel full dominance.

The hovering uncertainty about his eyes hardened into a frown; his mouth set hard. And it did not surprise the Bad Fellow to find that being in control once again felt, well, it felt good.

'Come with me,' he said to Felicity, pointing to a chest wrapped with chains, and they dragged it beside the boxes and crates and tables that were being piled up against the door. Cratchit was surprised out of congress with his inner demons by this display and rushed to bring any heavy objects he could find. Felicity too was impressed by Scrooge's new inward resolve, and while she moved briskly alongside Scrooge and displayed a surprising strength, this new regard brought a slight girlishness to her again whenever he spoke to her.

It took ten minutes for them to construct a barricade large enough that the door was so completely obscured they could no longer make out exactly where it had been, and realised to make the barricade larger still out of sheer guesswork might be to pointlessly fortify great stretches of wall.

They refilled their weapons a second, third, fourth time; tore holes in their clothes to improvise holsters for extra ones. Then there was little to do but wait, and try not to think. Nodger brought more wine and they drank again at the table, and the men smoked their pipes, and Felicity stole one of their pipes to have a smoke herself and, handing it back, pronounced the practice as disgusting as she had always supposed.

Mr Nodger produced still more wine, and perceiving that this was not the time to stand on ceremony, sat with them, and told them a joke that was at once exceedingly funny and also so very much more offensive than Tacker's worst outburst that the author finds himself powerless to include it here, even by the most circumscribed and delicate allusion. Zaltzwick himself, perhaps because he was so surprised to discover this talent in his footman after so many years of inexpressive servitude, or perhaps because half a life spent in the sober halls of Königsberg University left him unacquainted with ribald tales about the anatomy of barmaids, or, further, perhaps because he was spiritually weakened at that moment, laughed quite uncontrollably at it, until the rest of the group feared he was crying. When they were assured he was not, by a strange process the laughter spread through them as though it was an airborne infection, until not one could keep control of themselves or prevent the tears from flowing, except for Nodger, who maintained a serene composure.

As all parents know, when witnessing children in the full ferment of hilarity, the heights of excitement must be followed by a trough of some kind soon enough, and as the group drank still more wine and quietened after their laughter, a seriousness overtook them. The same spirit which had informed the servant that everything had changed and he would not still be employed the next morning in the same capacity he had been at dinner tonight, informed each of them that they only had an uncertain chance of seeing the morning at all. One by one, they crept away into other parts of the cavernous room to find a quiet moment to reflect, and make their peace with whatever and whoever they must, for what lay ahead.

Zaltzwick was particularly hard hit: it had finally occurred to him he was likely to die here, surrounded by his life's work, killed by the very things he had spent his life trying to protect against, and while these very researches were still unfinished, and he was unknown for them. Apparently without a God to consult, but only an incomplete corpus of results, theories, calculations and notes to flick through hollow-eyed, he remained at the table while the others disbanded into the shadows, to give him his moment alone.

As Scrooge walked into some far corner, and allowed his thoughts to drift through the childhood he had so long forgotten, until the ghosts had shown it to him, he found himself standing in front of Felicity.

'Mr Scrooge,' she began demurely, not meeting his eyes.

'My dear,' he said, surprised. 'The sight of you caught me unawares. I was shocked by—'

'By the sight of me,' she said.

'No. That is to say – yes. You reminded me of someone who was once quite dear to me.'

'Some maiden aunt with whiskers on her chin, no doubt,' said the pretty minx, whose chest beat hard with the wound of never once having provoked Scrooge to the mildest compliment, while she had callously rejected doughty military heroes for paying her just such a gift. 'Or some fat ugly wretch, or a moustachioed circus strongman with anvil tattoos upon his biceps?'

'Don't be silly,' he chided. 'A young lady with whom I was . . . connected. We were due to be married. I would say so with embarrassment, but I am too old to be embarrassed by such things now. Except that I suddenly thought of her, looking at you.'

The nook they found themselves in was exceedingly quiet and private, and a nearby ledge providing a natural seat, they sat alongside one another. Speaking quietly, they assumed an unexpected intimacy that was quite intoxicating.

'She died?' asked Felicity, taking Scrooge's hand.

'No indeed,' he said, although the vision he had seen earlier that evening confused him momentarily and made him pause long enough to pray his words were true. 'I was neglectful of her attention. And her *in*tentions, too. While I was concentrated on work, she married someone else and lived a very happy life, while I became a . . . well, never mind.'

'You missed out on love,' said Felicity, squeezing his hand harder. 'At first,' she corrected herself. Scrooge laughed out loud, and the girl, looking cross and upset with him, asked ingenuously, 'Why must you think it will stay that way?'

He laughed again. 'I would have been seventy within a few months.'

'Men grow stronger in spirit as they get older,' she attested, moving closer to him on the ledge.

'I am not suitable to start a family.'

'A rich man who is benefactor to all the neediest in his community. I cannot think of a better candidate,' she said, squeezing closer still.

'I shall,' he said, with a twinkly glance that declared this last remark would conclude the conversation, 'not very likely live out the night.'

'Then why wait?' she said, and instead of bounding into his lap, she pounced upon him and sat astride his legs.

'Good Lord . . .'

'We might be dead in a few minutes,' she said.

'I admit it,' he whispered, unsure what this all meant.

'These are our last moments together,' she said, making business with her skirts.

'It's true,' he insisted, all of a sudden determined to agree with her. A lifelong terror of female dress and anatomy was overthrown by an instant surge of energy and suddenly he was helping her with buttons and ties as angrily as one tearing off bonds after a long confinement. A strange bewildering energy took over his whole being and gave him a rapidity of movement matched by her own desperation to be rid of the seemingly endless layers of frilled cotton, each succeeded by another, more complicatedly fastened or elaborately frilled than the last, so that as they became excited by making progress into disrobement, they discovered themselves more complexly tied up in the process.

The couple did not allow this to get in the way of their excitement; indeed it increased it, and the more obstructions placed in their way by the layers of clothes, the harder they whispered encouragements of a most verbally innocent and yet usefully euphemistic kind. Their words became less euphemistic and more aggressively direct as the seconds went by until it became clear that Scrooge was so provoked he was only prevented from breaking verbal obscenity laws by his descriptive ignorance of female physical anatomy.

As in a bad dream, or a not quite good dream, they struggled for a good while (ten or fifteen seconds will seem a very long time in such a frustrated situation) and were so close to reaching a solution to their problem that it was in fact physically agonising when a noise interrupted them both, and forced them to collect themselves and scramble to rearrange their dress in case

someone might be nearby (where someone might easily have been all along, when they didn't care).

The disturbance, which brought all the others from the far corners of the great hall to seek each other out, was a sudden increased intensity in the groaning sound from outside, which for an hour or longer had been little more than a background hubbub. In just a few moments it had suddenly become so loud that none could ignore it, or fail to be frightened by it.

They gathered in the centre of the laboratory floor, all brought rudely and suddenly from their secret reflections, aware the time for those was now past.

'What has caused this?' asked Zaltzwick looking round at them desperately before turning his attention to the barricade which shivered visibly under some new attack. 'They are not simply gathered outside, they are *attacking* us! We are attracting them – why are they headed here? Surely none of us has become suddenly happy, that would be insane!'

'Yes, quite, of course . . .' said Felicity quickly.

'Impossible,' agreed Scrooge stiffly, attempting to stand behind Cratchit so he could hide his frustration and rebutton his flies.

Tacker caught sight of what Scrooge was doing and, forgetting his personal fears for a moment, his chest swelled with sincere pride. Covering for his friend, he said, 'Never mind that now. We must escape, that's all. Come on!' As he started to run away towards the tower staircase, the barricade shifted as though it were a mantle laid over a sleeping beast that was turning in its sleep.

'They have breached the door already,' said Zaltzwick despairingly. 'They are much stronger than I feared.'

'Trapped,' Cratchit was muttering, and rubbing his hand roughly over his face, as though he might succeed in waking himself up from this nightmare. 'Doctor!' he shouted. 'Why not release your creature? Henrietta! She could defend us against them!'

'No, no,' said Zaltzwick testily, 'she is quite stupid. She would probably kill us as well as they. And if she gets bitten, then she will turn zombie too. Ach, imagine that. We must retreat as fast as possible up the stairway and trust they do not follow us.'

The scientist was right: now that the creatures outside were roused, perhaps because there were so few remaining uninfected people in the area, the attack was becoming ferocious. Tacker and Cratchit heaved the crate of weapons up ahead of the group, who followed behind them. As they tumbled one by one up the staircase, Scrooge heard a crash of glass and splintered wood and looked back. It had only taken a handful of minutes for them to break through two heavy wooden doors. It afforded him a vertiginous lurch of horror to reflect that before that same amount of time had passed again, he might be dead.

It was too late to hide their route of escape. A few of the stumbling creatures had already seen them at the foot of the stairs, and were heading straight across towards them. But they were yet fifty yards away across the stone floor and Scrooge allowed his gaze to linger on them for a moment before he fled. A weird peace came over him, to look at those slow-moving, shambling forms, that seemed more absurd and mundane than they were frightening; many walked with twisted-around shoulders as though suffering from a hunched back or a crippling shyness. They looked comical and pathetic, and their progress was so slow as to add further comedy to it. It was an effort for Scrooge to persuade himself of the very imminent threat to his person and, yanking the door

closed behind him, he climbed the stairs to rejoin the group.

They were not far above, and had made a small
barricade with a grandfather clock, a chest and
several chairs.

'What's the plan here?' he demanded.

'It's not a complicated one. We kill as many as
we can and if we get overwhelmed, we move
further up the stairs and start again. But as short a
distance as possible. Because sooner or later we'll
run out of stairs.'

Reaching out to the hands he was offered,
Scrooge clambered over the barricade and
kneeling down on the other side, found a place
where he could comfortably lean, aim and shoot.
He heard the overturned grandfather clock's
laboured ticking beneath his arms and listened to
an entire minute click past, and discovered then
when you listened to an entire one without
moving, a minute was a huge expanse of time. He
thought of his whole life and the spirits who had
visited him; he thought of Felicity by his side. He
was fiercely determined to be alone with her
again, and for them to continue whatever it was
that they had been doing.

A multitude of dull thuds had fallen upon the

door, and it had emitted a number of squeaking noises to announce its intention of collapsing, before it finally broke down, and a crowd of openmouthed heads appeared below them. The group held fire as the initial wave of zombies had first to negotiate the feat of climbing stairs before they could present any actual danger. Tackling this challenge by simply falling flat on their faces, the first twenty or thirty formed a sloped carpet for the others behind them to climb.

When the closest face was but five feet away, they fired. The frail, bloodless skin and fragile bones of the creatures proved unexpectedly sensitive to gunshots and seemed to explode everywhere at once. Dead bodies that were inert fell back and shuddered to the floor between the crowd of those dead bodies that were still moving, who came on as fast as before.

Scrooge found his own aim true and unforgiving. He held a pistol in each hand and, taking half a second to aim, he fired; aimed; fired. All idea of sound was lost in the general noise. They could only see what was happening as if in silence and then through a thickening cloud of smoke that overwhelmed their sense of smell too, with its odour of burning. One after another heads were split in half, or burst right open, and desiccated

ONE AFTER ANOTHER HEADS WERE
SPLIT IN HALF, OR BURST RIGHT OPEN, AND
DESICCATED BRAINS FLEW UP

brains flew up and fell back down again like sloppy rain. Felicity and Tacker turned away to reload their guns, taking deep breaths. Cratchit was firing crazily, as they had expected he would when danger came at last, and missing with most of his shots. A few seconds later his twelve guns were all out of ammunition and he had to reload too.

Not an atom of light passed up from the room below, so crammed were the undead into that small stairwell, and the humans began to sense that as many as they might kill, so many hundreds more were pressing from below that the line could not be stopped. This thought struck a real mortal dread into them, as they saw a wall of dead bone and flesh rising towards them. They could not remain, but fled up the stairs, and stopping at the next corner, turned to improvise a more modest barricade and fire again.

As the horde below struggled to overcome the obstacles of furniture and grandfather clock, the jostling movement made the unmoving bodies filter to the floor like sediment to form a new carpet upon which the others could tread.

They came, leering and gawping, and reaching out with their insensible fingers towards the bullets that they did not understand were waiting for them.

Another volley struck them, broke their necks, smashed their heads, and propulsed gouting spurts of black slime in every direction, and once more the unmoving corpses at the front of the horde were pressed upwards by the force of the innumerable zombies below, and the human group retreated.

They had to move fast and Zaltzwick tripped, falling behind them, and then slipped on a trail of scattered intestines and skidded back to within reach of the arms below. They plucked at his coat; they grabbed him; one hand aiming for his eye accidentally removed his glasses as though it was a matter of form with them not to dine until such jewellery was removed; and with a diminishing cry of 'Hatstands!' in the air, they fell upon him ravenously.

The entrenched group above fired, and fired again. Scrooge did not miss once. His aim was precise, his reloading punctual, and when it came to retire further up the stairs he swept Felicity up brusquely and transported her in his arms, placing her down again with care, but with polite despatch. As he set her down for the third or fourth time, and before he could help improvise a barrier from the paltry materials to hand, his gun went off in his hand. The bullet smashed harmlessly into the wall by his side but the stock of his gun jumped back with the recoil, butting sharply against the side of his head, knocking all sense from it, and sending him at once into a reverie.

THE THIRD APPARITION

Scrooge swam down through dizzy thick clouds, as it seemed, until he saw that they were not metaphorical but were indeed clouds, and he was hovering high above a London that was burning. On every street buildings were on fire, and down every road crowds were running and screaming. There was a distant tap-tap of hurriedly assembled militias and newly-awoken regiments trying to form a beleaguered resistance with small arms. In the foreground, one structure dominated the landscape and he found himself focussing upon St Paul's, and on the figure of a lone young man on the roof, his clothes torn and in a panic, retreating from unseen assailants further and further up the dome, as far as he could go, until he was only a few feet short of the cross which stood at the very top. He was beside himself with fear, screaming for help that could not come.

Scrooge swam through the air, closer, until he saw that it was his beloved nephew. Now without his wife (presumably dead, or lost and alone), scared out of his wits, and shortly to die himself, either at the hands of the dreaded creatures, or by avoiding that fate plummeting to the ground either on purpose, or from misplacing a single footstep by the tiniest degree.

Scrooge felt a rush of air over him, and all turned black, as though a cloak had been thrown over his head, a cloak which was instantly pulled off again, to reveal that he was standing in a graveyard. In front of him stood a figure he knew too well. Tall, covered in a dark gown that obscured his face, and still as the night itself, stood the Ghost of Christmas Yet to Come.

'I believe I understand the message you are trying to give me,' he said to the Ghost.

The spirit, instead of replying, pointed ahead. In front of him Scrooge saw a deep and empty grave, or rather one that was not completely empty. A coffin had been placed in it, and a few dozen spadefuls of earth scattered over it, before for some reason the burial had apparently been abandoned.

'I should have known better than to expect an answer from you,' uttered Scrooge to the tall dark figure by his side. He couldn't help feeling that he was, at this point, a few steps ahead of the Three Spirits and the message they wanted to impart. They were trying to re-instil a sense of defensive cynicism in him, and cynically he had reached that conclusion first. 'I TELL you, sir,' he thus proceeded, 'you have nothing to teach me! I must return to my former wicked ways! I understand! I repent of my good and generous self and vow to be evil and grasping once more!'

The bony finger pointed again, urging Scrooge to look down at the coffin. He did so impatiently. A scratching noise came from within the coffin, and then a familiar creaking and cracking of wood. The earth shook. Scrooge sighed, quickly glanced at the name on the headstone and turned to the Ghost again.

'You're too LATE!' he said. 'You can't threaten me with death and turning into a zombie. I was already about a minute away from that when I passed out and was sent here!' There came no verbal response, which in Scrooge's experience of the Ghost of Christmas Yet to Come, was not a shattering surprise, but nevertheless finding himself standing around in this imaginary graveyard made Scrooge really lose his temper.

'You're thick as b—— pigswill, aren't you! Oh, to h— with this ...' and kicking the apparition as hard as he could between where he imagined the legs must be, and connecting painfully with what felt like a bony pelvis, he shoved the tall cloaked figure into the grave. It fell on top of the zombified version of himself that was breaking its way out of the coffin, presumably to scare him into some kind of action or teach him some lesson that for the moment he was content to ignore. Impatient to be back in the world and defending Felicity again, he stared at the grey sky, held his arms out and at the top of his voice demanded to be allowed to wake up. Which he did, with a start, to find he was still shouting.

VERSE IX

Ebenezer Scrooge did not allow the unexpected hiatus to prevent him from launching straight back into action, and making up for lost time. Felicity, who had been holding his head in her lap in fear it was permanently damaged, rose alongside him and they both aimed and fired their guns, in a movement of such harmony that you would have thought the splattering upward spray of blood and brains which greeted them was a firework celebration of their unity. When the current wave of dead bodies fell back, and Scrooge turned to reload, he demanded of Nodger:

'How far from the top of the staircase are we?'

'Not far, sir,' came the reply, and in Nodger's eye

he saw that the man craved forgiveness, as though he had just done something weak. Scrooge was confused, but then saw the man place the gun in his own mouth and pull the trigger. Angrily Scrooge turned away from the explosion and the falling body, the man already forgotten, and discharged his own gun with precision into the crowd. The humans who were left were tired and shaky, and missing with their guns more frequently as time went on. Cratchit's eyes were streaming and he was nearly insensible, in as much danger of shooting himself as he was anything else that moved.

The old Scrooge was most certainly back by now, but that same cold and calculating man perceived that an insane Cratchit was no help to his own and Felicity's survival. He grabbed Bob by the scruff of his neck and yanked him to his feet in the most sympathetic manner he knew.

'Now,' he said. 'Snap out of it, man! Get control of yourself.' His partner showed no signs of knowing him, but shook his head from side to side, gibbering. The only words Scrooge could make out were 'trapped' and 'hopeless'.

'Come, sir!' Scrooge shouted, and deemed it necessary to administer two sharp slaps across his face. 'Now! Be strong. You have everything to live for. A fine position. A huge and loving family who dote on you. Think of that. Think about Tiny Tim! How is the boy, by the way?'

Slowly a kind of recognition came back into the man's eyes, and he grabbed Scrooge's lapels harder even than his own were grabbed, until cloth was heard tearing. As he came into himself again the flame of anger was undimmed, though, but intensified, and so bursting with rage was he that he failed to get his words out, and gibbered still.

'Scrooge . . . Tim . . . Tiny . . .' he frothed at the mouth and his words tripped each other up until his eye slipped from Scrooge's own and fell upon the advancing pack that scrambled stupidly on the stairs below. A terrible recognition dawned in those eyes as he made something out in the thronging mass, and he pointed as though transfixed by a revenging spectre.

'There!' he shouted. 'There he is!'

And there indeed he was. A full head above any of the other zombies, tall and lumbering, as close to muscular as any of those things could be, Tiny Tim rose towards them from the middle of the crowd, his teeth snapping, his pale dead eyes set in a mean wolfish glare, as though through some mystical agency his spirit was able to comprehend what he was doing, and loved every second of it. He bore up towards them, clawing the air, and this sight tipped Cratchit finally and irrevocably over the edge.

'It's you!' he cried. 'The bane of my life! I knew you would come! I've been waiting for you!' He pulled a gun from each pocket and placed a large dagger under his arms. He turned to wish Felicity and Scrooge good luck in words that were lost in the gunfire. Then he threw himself down into the throng, screaming the vilest oaths and curses, firing shots that tore holes in Tiny Tim's chest, and burst open his belly, and blew out one of his eyes, and blasted one hand into fragments. Cratchit fell beneath his son's zombified corpse. For a moment they could see him, hacking away with the blade until the head was nearly severed. Then he was subsumed beneath the rising tide.

They fired, reloaded, fired again. Scrooge picked Felicity up and she continued firing the shotgun over his shoulder as he carried her aloft. Tacker kept shooting tirelessly, but at last they could see he too knew there was nothing to be done: they could postpone, but not avoid the attack. At last they came to a roof with a trapdoor in it, and scrambling through they pulled it shut, and sat upon it.

They found themselves outside and high up, on a small crenellated balcony in which they saw the final certainty of their fate. For it was enclosed, and abutted no other building, and there was now, to be sure, no escape. The night air tasted sweet in their mouths, and Felicity slid sideways to lie on the floor, sweating profusely and breathing hard. Around them the sky was clear and snowed-out, and the stars sparkled in happy ignorance of the events they shone down upon. Scrooge appreciated that here was one last moment of peace and beauty, but the man who would have been glad to see it was dead within him.

'Merry Christmas,' he said to Tacker.

The American nodded. 'It's been nice dying with you, man.'

'Dying?' said Felicity, sitting up. 'But they have to climb a ladder to reach this door, and they have no way of doing that. We are safe, aren't we?'

'My dear, I would love to deceive you, but alas you would soon discover why this was not true. No, I would not describe us as safe. You saw how they climbed on the corpses of their fallen brethren? And how those behind pushed them forward relentlessly? They will continue to come, and clamber over each other until they break out into here. I daresay they will continue until they are tumbling off this parapet in their hundreds.'

He gathered her to him to give her temporary comfort, or to apologize for delivering her this news. When she was resting against his chest, she nodded. 'It *is* all over then. I must say, I apologize for my aunts. They can be hard to chivvy at times.'

'Young lady, don't mention it. I'm sorry we didn't save them. Not that we would have been able to,' said Tacker, lighting a cigar. 'Smoke?'

'Never too late to start, I suppose,' said Scrooge, accepting.

'Filthy habit,' said a voice.

'I know,' agreed Scrooge.

'Never catch me doing that,' said the voice.

'The sentiment does you great credit,' answered Scrooge.

The soft and gentle voice presently coughed with a great deal of polite embarrassment and paused before piping up once more. 'If you will excuse me the very great offence of interrupting your conversation, gentlemen, may I offer you a lift?'

While he had been conversing with it, Scrooge had presumed the voice to be Felicity's. So utterly alien for him was the sensation of having another person's head resting against his chest, he was quite innocent of the fact that were the voice hers, he would feel a pleasing little reverberation every time she spoke. So as he realised the voice was not hers, instead of behaving like the stealthy warrior that Scrooge considered himself to be at that moment, he and Tacker leapt up and Felicity, who had ebbed into a shallow slumber now the excitement was past, was unavoidably woken by this movement, and the three of them stared up at the enormous shape that bobbed above them, of a hot air balloon.

'Good Lord,' said Mr Scrooge, 'it's Mr Peewit. Sir, I never thought I should be glad to see you. Let me shake you by the hand.'

'Best not,' replied that stout gentleman, who was finding it hard to remain steady as it was, leaning over the side of the basket of his balloon. 'I say,' he remarked, 'one of you catch this rope, or I might drift away.'

They did so, and to Mr Peewit's surprise they set about securing it in a great hurry, and wasted no time in small talk. Before he had much of a chance to steady the contraption against the side of the tower, Scrooge had thrown his lady friend in head first, scrambled in after, and then helped the large American man to follow them.

'You're very welcome, you know,' said Peewit,

beaming with pride to have them aboard. 'Delighted for the company, to be honest. Have been sailing over the city for hours. Wonderful views . . .'

Leaning past him and making no attempt to avoid knocking him clean out of the balloon's basket, Scrooge roughly untied the rope that fastened them to the tower, and slung it away into the air. To the exquisite anxiety of all aboard (except for their exceptionally rich and dull-witted captain), the balloon remained quite still for a moment and hung there as though nothing else could be expected of it, before some silent breeze took hold of it, and swung it first a few gentle feet away and then, taking a firmer grip, lifted them up into the night air. It was just in time and they looked down at the trapdoor as it began to rattle, and then opened a few inches, fingers appearing around the sides.

'Funny business,' said Peewit, pouring himself a glass of champagne. 'But there seems to be an awful lot of commotion in the streets tonight, what? Celebration and shouting, and I'm afraid quite a few fights too. Not an edifying sight. But still, Christmas, eh? You stare at me, sir.' Thus he apostrophized the festive Mr Scrooge, for that gentleman had indeed fixed upon him a look of such frowning intensity that only one who had lived a life entirely filled with joy and free of disapprobation (as Mr Peewit had) could fail to feel physically endangered by it.

'You mean, you were up here by *coincidence*?' Scrooge asked, gripping the sides of the basket and shaking, contemplating how unlikely their rescue had been, after all.

'Well no, I was up here on purpose, dear boy. I wasn't sleep-ballooning, you know? Why, what do you mean?'

'Why, you d——ed idiot, can't you see for yourself? The streets are teeming with homicidal maniacs! We were nearly eaten alive!'

Peewit pressed his spectacles to the top of his nose and took a sip of champagne. 'Are you sure they meant to eat you?' he asked. 'It seems rather extreme behaviour. Surely some sort of misunderstanding, I should say?'

Felicity was stood next to the kindly Mr Peewit, and had been regarding him in the light of a great saviour who had come out of the heavens, which although he was exactly that, in her gratitude he had taken on altogether a more celestial glow. Even her happiness, however, could not withstand the man's exasperating stupidity and grasping him by

193

the lapels, she lifted him bodily off the ground and brought his face forward until it was but a few millimetres from her own.

'It is not a misunderstanding,' she said in a determined way which demanded his agreement. 'Our friends have been killed in front of us. Torn apart. We have watched them being eaten.'

'Oh dear,' said Mr Peewit weakly.

'The city is being devoured from the inside.'

'This *is* bad news,' offered the balloonist.

'The dead are rising from their graves.'

'Poor show,' he whispered.

'And we have endured several hours in their company.'

'Most exasperating.'

'So I suggest you believe us.'

'I offer my sincerest condolences. If I had a hat, I would take it off out of respect.'

Returning him to his feet, Felicity's irritation somewhat appeased, she pointed out, 'You do have a hat.'

'Ah, indeed. Then . . .' and with an extraordinarily over-elaborate display of grace he removed the item from his head, twiddled it in the air six or seven times and then performed a deep bow, to the inconvenience and complete puzzlement of the other two men in the balloon's basket, who were obliged to get out of the way. 'My lady, I am so very sorry for your trouble, and I exult in the privilege of being the agent of your escape. And perhaps we shouldn't land at Richmond, if that is the case, but head out to my country seat.'

'Where's that?' asked Scrooge.

'The village of Little Puddlecombe. Charming spot. Picked it up for a song.'

'The manor house, you mean?'

Peewit coughed modestly. 'Well, the whole village, in fact. But the manor house came with it. Handsome building, high battlements, and stocked for the whole winter. Ah, talking of stocks! Now!' He clapped his hands and opened the hamper at his feet.

'I have goose liver pate and a game pie, mustard and potted horseradish sauce to go with the sliced beef. But – silly me! – you'll want champagne first, and I've got some cold punch if you don't . . .'

As the little fellow busied himself with the duty of being a host, the other two men looked out at the night. Now the excitement had passed, the cold was quite disagreeable, and they both hugged themselves and kept their own counsel.

Scrooge remained lost in his thoughts, looking

down, as Peewit offered him a glass of champagne. He had accepted it before he paid attention to what it was, and handed it back. 'No, thanks,' he said. 'Have you got any brandy?'

'Too late! You've touched it so you've got to drink it!' giggled Peewit. 'But ah – how about a tot of brandy to make it a champagne cocktail? Now – there you go. Surely this is the most civilized balloon ride you've been in this year, Mr Scrooge?'

Making no comment, Scrooge sipped his drink (which was admittedly a reviving concoction), and looked over the side again, pondering whether death at the hands of the zombies might be less excruciating than spending a few hours in a small balloon basket with this dementedly jolly companion. Peering down into the streets below (they were now above Holborn Hill) he saw something which arrested all his other thoughts.

'Good Lord,' he muttered, and touched the elbow of his American friend to gain his attention.

'Wow,' said Mr Tacker. 'Will you look at that?'

They both leaned out as far as they could and watched the street far below, down which thousands of the undead monsters were wandering in a thick crowd. With the disinterested fascination of children looking down on a huge swarm of ants from a balcony, they witnessed the zombies pursue the balloon's trail down Kingsway, and round Aldwych, and onto the Strand.

'Definitely following us,' said Scrooge. 'Do you think the happiness theory still stands?' They both turned and regarded Mr Peewit, who was at that moment opening another bottle of champagne and telling Felicity all about the remarkable collection of shooting guns housed at his new country manor.

'I am assured it is the finest display of such weapons in all England,' he boasted in his piping little voice. 'And now, I know, my dear, that guns are perfectly beastly things, but one's friends do so enjoy shooting partridge and pheasant, and one does so enjoy eating them oneself, you know?'

'G— d— it, why did I try to bring guns to sell to the British?' Tacker drawled lifelessly, and as Scrooge's sympathetic glance settled upon him he saw a light come into those eyes, which had been absent for several hours, as though that initial thought connected to another more useful one, and then that to an even more exciting idea still.

'Scrooge!' he whispered, 'I've got a plan. Where are we now?'

'Near the top of the Strand – look, there's Drury Lane. My goodness, they can't still be playing

Hamlet: The Musical? I was asked to invest in that, I could have made a bomb—'

'Shut up! A bomb is exactly what we *are* going to make. Listen. My ship is moored not far from here, and it's packed with explosives . . .' He whispered the rest of his plan into Scrooge's ear, and the Englishman at once agreed that they had to act quickly.

'Mr Peewit,' asked Scrooge, with an air of casual enquiry, 'how does one steer this thing?'

'Well, it's not easy, you know,' he said. 'Takes a good deal of practice, but one can pull on these ropes to allow hot air out so we go down . . .' As he explained the rudiments to Scrooge, out of politeness to what he assumed was some sort of American Christmas game, Mr Peewit affected not to notice that Tacker was winding a thick rope around his right leg until it was bound fast. The end of the rope was tied to his ankle with a final flourish, and the instructions on flying the balloon similarly tied up, Mr Peewit raised his spectacles to examine his foot, and was going to make a remark along the lines of what fun it was to enjoy such japes at Christmastime, and weren't they all having such a wonderful flight together, when the gravity in the other men's eyes gave him pause. He saw that the rope attached to his foot ran over the side of the balloon, and looped back up again to be fixed to one of the wooden hoops for that purpose, and he had a presentiment that gravity of another sort was about to become his presiding concern.

'Mr Peewit, you are a kind man,' began Scrooge.

'I thank you sir,' said the other, smiling, nodding his head and nearly falling over.

'A generous host.'

'I certainly do my best.'

'And you always have your guests' best interests at heart.'

'It gives me great pleasure that you acknowledge the fact,' said Peewit, and in that heart which Scrooge had mentioned swelled a great happiness and pride.

'So I'm sorry for what we are about to do, but you must trust us it is to help us all out of this predicament.'

To their surprise, Charles Peewit made no protest, but stood as nobly as that great monarch, his namesake, once stood on the steps of the scaffold. He nodded, and even then, in full knowledge of what was about to happen, the trace of a smile could not be eradicated from his lips.

'Sorry, chum,' said Tacker, choosing this moment

to employ some local slang (to the complete bafflement of the aristocrat who he was about to manhandle) and, heaving Peewit up over his shoulders, tipped him overboard. There was a thump of sorts as he came to rest, and the basket jostled mightily for a second before regaining its equilibrium.

Felicity had been watching this conversation with a frown, and as Peewit disappeared over the side, sprang to Scrooge's side, and tried to pull him back up.

'What are you *doing*?' she asked. 'You *b—s*!'

'Look,' pointed Scrooge. Peering down into the Strand, Felicity saw the many thousands of zombies, packing the thoroughfare from side to side, all following the progress of the balloon.

'He's like a beacon to them,' said Scrooge. 'If Tacker is right, and there are enough explosives on his boat, then perhaps we can lure them close enough, and possibly clear London of this plague.'

Felicity nodded sadly as soon as she was satisfied of their reasons, and called down below: 'Are you all right, Mr Peewit?'

'Oh yes!' came back the quite cheerful voice. 'There goes my hat, whoopsidaisy. No champagne spilt up there, I hope?'

'No, none!' Scrooge shouted back.

FELICITY CALLED DOWN BELOW: 'ARE YOU ALL
RIGHT, MR PEEWIT?'

'Jolly good. I say, this is rather fun, don't you know?'

'Keep your spirits up!' called Scrooge to him, taking control of the vessel as best he could. In truth he made but little difference to its course, but luck instead guided them the short distance until they saw Waterloo Bridge, and a thick crowd surging from the south to meet the even larger one already gathered at the north end beneath the balloon.

'Stop it. Can you make it stop?' asked Tacker. They were nearly over the boat now and Scrooge let out all the air he could, to lower their height and slow their progress.

'Can you grab the railings, Mr Peewit?' called down Scrooge. 'We must affix ourselves to the ship, everything depends on it. Catch hold!'

'Righto!' called up the friendly voice, quite unfazed. 'Throw me a rope and I'll tie it. Getting quite close, I'll make contact any second- OW!'

As they saw him catch hold, they threw him all the ropes they could find and with his help they were soon tied to the side of the ship in three or four places, although the wind was dragging them hard to starboard, so that the balloon leant at a desperate angle. Mr Peewit, noticing that the zombie creatures were beginning to fall onto the ship's deck and correctly surmising that he would be no use in battling against them while he hung upside down with a huge knot tied around his ankle, cast off from the ship and hung once more perpendicular from balloon out above the water, whistling his old school song.

'Now,' said Tacker, and he pulled a small metal canister from inside his coat. The others did not know what this could be, but he explained it was the prototype of an incendiary device. 'I had no way of using it before,' he said, 'without putting ourselves in danger. Now's my chance.'

Priming the chemical device (as he explained) by removing the pin, he aimed for the gap which led down into the hold of his boat where the explosives were stored, and threw. But with the balloon listing at the end of a sixty-foot rope, it was an impossible shot, as Scrooge and Felicity had known the second he said he was going to try it. With an impressive force, he managed to throw it so it clattered onto the deck and exploded loudly and impressively enough for them to have to shield their eyes.

'Phew-ee!' called Peewit from below.

But the boat was largely unharmed. Showing themselves as mad with hunger as they had been before, more than ten thousand of the creatures were now crammed into the nearest part of the bridge, crushing each other against the rails so that bodies were cut in half and torsos were thrown down onto the deck where they propelled themselves along with their arms, still working their jaws and chewing the air, while hundreds more full-bodied ones followed them.

'I know what I have to do,' said Tacker solemnly. There was no protest from Scrooge or Felicity, nor could they think of anything whatever to say. Possibly every zombie in London was now gathered in this one place, and they had a final chance to make this blow against them. Before the others could formulate a reply, Mr Tacker had swung himself out onto the rope and was climbing down it, hand over hand, until he was on the deck.

The creatures swarmed over the rails even faster at the sight of him there, falling in their hundreds, as many into the river (where they helplessly sank) or crushed by the fall onto the deck, as there were those who got up or struggled along on broken limbs, trying to chase Tacker. He skirted the flames caused by the useless bomb, and stood at the prow, priming a second device and keeping it in his hand over the gap above the hold, in which he had said were hundreds of tonnes of explosives. He let the creatures get as close as he dared, until there were perhaps two or three thousand zombies on the ship, and from a distance it seemed as though it seethed with maggots. At last Tacker waved towards the balloon, smiled briefly, pulled the trigger of the bomb, and let go.

It only occurred to Scrooge as he saw Tacker drop it that not only was he about to see the most spectacular fireworks display London had played host to since the Great Fire, but that they were much too dangerously close to it. Launching himself at the hamper, and finding there a carving knife, he was hacking desperately at the cords attaching them to the ship when he heard an explosion. The bomb had exploded, and Ebenezer caught a last sight of Tacker being set upon by creatures, fighting them off with a gun in either hand. He made out a distant cry of:

'F— yeah! Take that you f—ing c—sucking motherf—ing a—holes! Suck my—' before the last thread of the rope snagged on the blade, tore free and the balloon lurched violently in the wind. It swung away with force as gravity corrected itself, and was then buffeted by a far more violent burst of wind, instantly followed by a terrific roar that seemed to encompass the whole world. Scrooge and Felicity were forced against the side of the basket hard enough to knock the wind from them, and then thrown higgledy-piggledy from side to side among a debris of champagne bottles, loaded shotguns, pats of butter, meat pies, muskets, cutlery, puddings, and the stuffed head of a wildebeest.

Scrooge righted himself and clutched hard at the side of the basket, peering out to see the damage, and found it hard to make anything out in the huge plume of smoke and the debris falling in a wide circle, making a shockingly beautiful pattern in the air and splashing down, as though it was some demonic fountain built to worship the god of destruction itself, spraying burning wood and shattered rock. Such was the strength of the explosion, air rushed around them like a hurricane as the balloon was swept away. Already far in the distance, Scrooge caught a brief glimpse of the site of the explosion: the bridge, with a hole as though a gargantuan bite had been taken out of it by a mythic beast of the ocean, cast across with flaming wreckage and still bodies. The ship was torn in half and was sinking so quickly that it was now scarcely visible, its two ends no taller above the frothing waves than two thatched cottages – and now it was gone entirely. Not one moving figure did he see there.

'Mr Peewit!' said Felicity.

Scrooge pulled in the rope and his hopes sank faster than the balloon rose in the air, for it was too light, and before he had taken it in to half its length, he found in his hands a frayed and cindered collection of threads where thick stout rope should be, and beyond that, nothing. He was sick and dizzy, and had not the heart to tell Felicity, but she saw what was in his hands. They both subsided weakly on the floor again, and sitting there with each other in their arms were rocked by the motion of the wind, and the corresponding motion of the basket, and the not unconnected forward and backward motion of their thoughts, until they slept.

AN
EPILOGUE

Mr Scrooge woke upon Christmas Day to find himself quite a different man from the one who had woken twenty-four hours earlier. Instantly upon waking, he knew what day it was, yet he did not smile. He saw the bright blue sky above and all around, and did not take a breath of fresh air and thank the Lord that he was alive.

The Scrooge who would have done such things was dead. And worse, he was a fool. Instead, Scrooge threw the blanket off himself and replaced it with care around the shoulders of Felicity, and set about tidying their confined space so that it didn't, as he inwardly remarked, look like a Spanish wedding had occurred in it. He placed the food items back in the

hamper, and the armaments stacked next to each other in the corner. He cleaned all of the ammunition he could find and placed it within the correct guns, after he had cleaned the guns themselves, and then, having brushed the wicker floor as best he could and thrown the crumbs out into the air for the birds and field mice to make their Christmas breakfast upon them (if they must), prepared a meagre breakfast of cold roast chicken, cold potatoes and mustard, and bread-and-marmalade, which (having gently roused his companion with encouraging words) they washed down with a bottle of cider.

Then they looked out from their extraordinary vantage point, over a view neither would ever have expected to witness. Below and ahead of them stretched mile after mile of countryside, blanketed white by a foot-deep snowfall, the morning so young that not a single footprint yet blemished that perfect covering, and it was as though the very world had fallen asleep, never to wake, and been left for them alone. Felicity laid her head peacefully upon Scrooge's arm, and he drew the blanket around her again, wary of the cold's effect upon her young frame, after the previous night's excitements.

It was in the character of his old self to be

content to remain unspeaking for hours at a time, and only to watch and look out for the best for himself in every situation, and calculate the surest way of getting the greatest outcome. Felicity seemed to understand this, and not to expect him to speak. Yet now something aroused him from his grim and content silence and made him look more closely at the hills and valleys that wound away below them.

'I'll be d———,' he said and, reaching up, yanked on the rope that released hot air from the top of the contraption, and made them dip nearer to the earth. 'It is!' he muttered presently as he got a closer view, and causing a further huge gulp of air to escape by another tug on the rope they lurched downwards.

'Hold on!' he said, clutching her close and pulling on the rope once more, this time with such force that almost all the air escaped from the balloon in one breath. The contraption plummeted sharply, pitched with a crash against the stone battlement of a building, turned on its end and emptied them with remarkable efficiency (and a certain amount of bruising) onto a turret, a much wider and grander kind than the one which they had escaped a few hours previously.

The balloon continued its journey, and seemed

likely to pull half the wall away in its efforts to drag
the huge basket along with it, so seizing a grapefruit
knife from the ground beside him Scrooge attacked
the ropes until it was freed. The basket fell back and
sat up pertly, and the freed balloon, now no longer a
perfect sphere but a wobbling, buxom approximation
of one, bounced away across the treetops of the
nearby woods, looking no larger than a child's play-
ball, and producing the illusion that the trees, and
church spire, and background of hills against which
it was viewed, were no larger than a very detailed
setting for a child's doll's house.

'This is Peewit's mansion,' said Scrooge. 'I can't
believe it. Almost as though the balloon found its
way here by force of habit.'

'He said it's abandoned, didn't he?' asked Felicity,
trying the door down from the roof, and surprised
to find it open.

'No – shut up for the winter, but ready for
guests,' said Scrooge, happily rubbing his hands.
'Knowing him, I expect I know what that means.
Plenty of food stored away in the ice-house, lots of
good wine.'

'And guns,' she said innocently. 'He mentioned
guns.'

He had indeed mentioned them. And as Felicity

212

went about the house (cautioned strongly from unlocking any of the ground-floor shutters or doors except the small servant's entrance at the back) he brought all of these weapons one by one to the landing beneath the roof. He moved every last round of ammunition there too. He established an armed-and-ready arsenal and moved three dozen of the best weapons (which made up scarcely ten per cent of the entire collection) up onto the ramparts of the manor house to look down on the grounds from every angle.

Felicity understood that he needed to feel safe, but for her own part wanted only to feel the snow under her feet and have a look at the local environs, to get the evil sights of the previous night out of her mind by walking through the wide bright fields that surrounded the great house. It seemed she could see for miles, just from the front lawn. She knew that the horrors of the last day would be with her for years, would probably never be truly vanquished, but in this moment the natural beauty of her surroundings, the architectural grandeur of the house and grounds were like she had not seen before, and her luck at having escaped all combined to cause a feeling of miraculous deliverance and pure, natural happiness.

And now she saw people coming over the fields towards her. They had seen the balloon, and were coming to see if there were survivors, or if they could help. From the woods half a mile away she saw them come one by one, and she felt happier still.

'Hello!' she called out, even though she knew they wouldn't be able to hear her. 'Hello!' She waved out of sheer joy to see other humans, and waved, and waved. A few seconds later she noticed they were not yet much closer. They didn't seem to be running. She turned and trotted back to the house.

'Some people are coming to help us!' she called up to Scrooge on the battlements above. 'Can you see them?'

He didn't answer her at first, but disappeared from view. He came back a few seconds later, and laid out another half-dozen guns from under his arm, over the edge of the battlements. 'To help us,' he said. 'Humbug. Humbug, my dear.'

'Mr Scrooge?' she asked, and turned back to look at the locals who had wandered out of the forest. It was curious that they still didn't seem to be much closer, and quite a few of those she could make out seemed to walk with limps.

'Come inside, my dear,' he said, not looking at her, but out over the fields, 'and fetch yourself a gun.

Merry Christmas. We've got a fine morning's killing to do.' She had already disappeared inside the servant's entrance by the time he finished his sentence, and he was left alone, cocking gun after gun, and holding one of the rifles up to his shoulder to see if the first one of them was yet within range. He smiled as a thought occurred to him, of a phrase he had once heard used in earnestness, and which now rang nasty and hollow, and without thinking he voiced his own version of it.

'God save us,' he said quietly, maintaining his aim dead straight across the fields. He laughed in that mean low chuckle that had not been heard by anyone for many years. 'God save us, every one.'

Patrick Jackson is an artist and illustrator
whose work has been exhibited in the
Britain, the United States and France.
www.jackson-art.com